Stucksville

A MELANIE KROUPA BOOK

Stucksville

Sheila Greenwald

DORLING KINDERSLEY PUBLISHING, INC.

A Melanie Kroupa Book

Dorling Kindersley Publishing, Inc.

95 Madison Avenue

New York, New York 10016

Visit us on the World Wide Web at http://www.dk.com

Dorling Kindersley books are available at special discounts for bulk
purchases for sales promotions or premiums. Special editions, including
personalized covers, excerpts of existing guides, and corporate imprints
can be created in large quantities for specific needs. For more information,
contact Special Markets Dept., Dorling Kindersley Publishing, Inc.,
95 Madison Ave., New York, NY 10016; fax: (800) 600-9098.

Library of Congress Cataloging-in-Publication Data

Greenwald, Sheila.

Stucksville / Sheila Greenwald. — 1st ed.

p. cm. "A DK Ink book."

Summary: While working on a project for a contest at school,
fourth grader Emerald comes to appreciate her family's very small, cramped
New York City apartment.

ISBN 0-7894-2675-7 [1. Apartment houses—Fiction. 2. New York (N.Y.)—
Fiction. 3. Contests—Fiction. 4. Schools—Fiction.] I. Title. PZ7.G852 St 2000

[Fic]—dc21 00-029476

Book design by Jennifer Browne.

The illustrations for this book were drawn using pen and ink.

The text of this book is set in 13 point Garamond.

Printed and bound in U.S.A.

First Edition, 2000

2 4 6 8 10 9 7 5 3 1

In gratitude for
the Museum of the City of New York

Contents

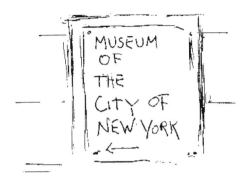

Outta-Here Emerald

"Emerald, are you okay?" Angel jostled her classmate's arm.

"Fine, fine." Emerald Costos tried to sound normal, even though she could barely speak.

Emerald and Angel stood side by side in front of a glass case in a dimly lit gallery on the third floor of the Museum of the City of New York. All around them, classmates from Mrs. Alter's fourth grade at P.S. 112 were pointing at the cases and talking excitedly to one another. Inside the cases were dollhouses, some of them over one hundred years old. Each house was filled with

1

dozens of perfect tiny things.

Angel began to read from the large print on the side of the case. "'This house was made as a teaching toy to instruct the girls of the family in the care of household objects.'"

To Emerald, the house seemed less like a teaching toy than a small miracle—serene, tidy, and secure.

"Boy, that's rich people lived there." Manuel Estrada nudged Emerald aside for a better view.

"I wonder if they were happy," Hector Torres whispered.

"Oh, they were happy," Emerald assured him.

"How would you know?" Angel challenged her.

"I can imagine it," Emerald said, imagining it.

Angel rolled her eyes. "For all we know *you* live in a dollhouse. Maybe that's why you never invite anybody over, including people in your building who invited you."

"We're redecorating," Emerald mumbled. It was her mother's favorite excuse.

"Redecorating since September?" Angel hooted. "My pop says your place is a shoe box, and your folks could redecorate just by using a broom."

Emerald felt herself getting almost small enough

to crawl inside the dollhouse in front of her. How could it be that she had the bad luck to live across the courtyard from big-mouth Angel Montero, whose father, the building super, had come to check a leaky faucet on the worst morning of a messy week?

"That time when your father came," she explained, "we all had stomachaches."

"My pop," Angel continued as if she hadn't heard, "he says you eat takeout off a suitcase."

"There isn't much room."

"So how come you don't take over the whole apartment? The lady who lives in the front part, she's not coming back from the nursing home. Soon the place will be up for rent. Your folks could reconnect the rooms like it used to be. Front to back."

"We won't be here that long."

"You told me. What was that song you sang? Oh, yeah, 'I should worry, I should care. In another year, I'm outta here.'"

"That's right." Emerald nodded.

"So where are you going, Outta-Here Emerald?"

"Someplace." Emerald shrugged, not adding that it couldn't be far enough or soon enough.

She didn't see why she had to explain to Angel that her parents were actors who had moved half a dozen times since she was born, from one theater to another, until a great offer had brought them to New York, only to fall through at the last minute. She didn't have to tell her the "suitcase" was a metal camp trunk they had found at a Goodwill Store. It was not only a table but a closet that contained all their summer clothes.

Mrs. Alter clapped her hands. "Okay, okay, everybody," her voice rang out. "Another group is coming through, and we want a little time downstairs in the gift shop."

They formed a line and shuffled out of the darkened room, past cases of teddy bears and lady dolls and clothes made in France, moving into the elevator and then down to the bright shop full of books and toys and games.

Emerald's classmates grabbed at bead kits and postcards and paper dolls.

"Okay, okay, everybody. Make your decisions quickly." Mrs. Alter was always in a rush. "See if you can find something that will help you with your My New York project, which is due in just a few weeks. It would be nice if someone from our school won the citywide essay contest and got to meet the mayor. The three best essays will be read in our own school assembly. Don't forget to tell your parents the date."

At the thought of the My New York project, Emerald's stomach knotted. She still hadn't come up with a topic. What was her New York anyway? Her mind went blank. It was no more *her* New York than it had been *her* Louisville or Minneapolis or Duluth or any of the other places her parents had gone to work with high hopes and big dreams. Only a few days before, she had heard Niko, her father, say, "The Water Gap Theater is interested. They offer a full-year contract. And if they like you they may renew it."

Renew it? Emerald tried to imagine what it might be like to stay in one place for more than a year.

"Finally, we could really settle in one spot," Niko said. "They want us to audition here, then fly down and take a look at the theater."

By this time next year, Emerald thought, she could be working on an assignment entitled My Water Gap. Niko seemed to think this move would be different. Would it?

"Emerald, you're the only one in the class without a purchase." Mrs. Alter's voice interrupted her daydream.

"I don't want anything," she murmured.

The trip mother, Mrs. Lauffer, smiled gently. "Guthry can't decide what to buy either," she said about her son, who hung back from the displays. Guthry and his parents and older brother Lenny lived on the first floor of Emerald's building. Guthry was called "class artist" because his notebooks had drawings where homework should have been. His comics were so good that classmates offered to pay if Guthry would draw them as superheroes. What amazed Emerald was that Guthry could capture a person's face on paper without ever seeming to look at him.

"I can help you out with a few dollars." Mrs. Lauffer reached into her purse.

"No, thanks," Emerald said, shaking her head. People often offered to help her, even people who were hard up themselves. It had something to do with being skinny and pale and, as her mother said, "the only little kid I've ever known, except for myself when I was your age, with dark circles under her eyes."

Her mother was Darcy, who went by her first name to everyone, including Emerald. She was slender now, not skinny, and expert at powdering over the circles above and below her eyes to make her lovely face lovelier.

Emerald couldn't wait to tell her about the dollhouses.

"Oh, the dollhouses," Darcy exclaimed when Emerald described the class trip while they ate their dinner of pizza and salad. "My parents took me to see them on a visit to the city when I was your age. I would dream of making myself small enough to fit inside." She laughed. "I should have worked harder at getting small. Look where I ended up."

Emerald didn't have to look. She knew by heart the back half of the divided apartment called a railroad flat because it was shaped like a train car. "I'll bet Water Gap will have more space," she guessed.

"Even Five-C would have more space if it hadn't been divided in two," Darcy said.

"Angel Montero says that Mrs. Riley isn't coming back from the nursing home. She says we could knock down the dividing wall and take the whole place. That would give us a window on the street."

Darcy shuddered. "It's bad enough having to *live* on this block, let alone *look* at it. Thank goodness this is just a stopping-off place. When we get our big break, we'll be on our way."

"Hooray for Water Gap!" Emerald cheered, not quite sure what she was cheering about. Another move or Darcy's enthusiasm or just to show what a trouper she was.

"Or something closer." Darcy winked mischievously, surprising Emerald. She leaned over the pizza, her face glowing with excitement. "If we get our break right here . . . who knows?" She wiped her fingers on a napkin and reached behind her to the stack of real-estate catalogs she loved to collect. "Let's take a look."

The catalogs were kept on top of some unused cookbooks on the kitchen wall of what they called the Everything Room. It *was* everything— the kitchen, living room, and Niko and Darcy's bedroom all in one. Just down a short hallway was a bathroom and Emerald's bedroom, which

Darcy called Cubby with Cot. Both the Everything Room and Cubby with Cot looked out on a courtyard with facing windows, a brick wall, and a fire escape. An old gray shade that Darcy jokingly called their window treatment was kept drawn night and day, allowing in only the dimmest light.

Darcy opened a crisp new catalog from Luxury Properties Limited. "It's a good thing Niko is at work," she confided. "You know how he feels about these."

Niko waited on tables at Baxter's Steak House most nights of the week, leaving his days free to search for a real job as an actor. He said the catalogs were pie in the sky and it did Darcy no good to read them.

"Niko is wrong," Darcy insisted, flipping the glossy pages. "It's not pie in the sky to think that one day we could live in places like these. I'm in and out of these buildings all the time on my catering jobs. They are full of people just like us, only they've had a break. Just because Niko's part in *I'll Take Manhattan* and my soap opera role fell through doesn't mean a thing. It's only a matter of time till something terrific happens. I can feel it. Overnight, our lives could change, the way they did for our drama school buddies Ted and Martha."

Pulling out a catalog, she continued, "A new apartment for us, private school for you." She pointed to a photo of a town house only blocks away. "I've catered at this one. It's got a garden and a sauna."

They were so absorbed in the photographs that neither of them heard Niko's key in the lock. They weren't even aware he was in the room until he was beside them doing his *peck-peck* chicken-imitation kisses that always made Emerald laugh.

Darcy tried to slip the catalog back on the pile, but Niko saw it and frowned. "Danger," he said, shaking his head.

"Emerald told me about her class trip to see the dollhouse models at the Museum of the City of New York," Darcy began quickly. "It reminded me of this mansion. I was *not* daydreaming pie in the sky."

"Oh, no?" Niko exclaimed with exaggerated disbelief.

"No," Darcy insisted. "Five-C is okay."

"C for convenient." Niko nodded. "I'm glad you appreciate a kitchen so close to the bedroom that not only can you eat breakfast in bed, you can prepare it from bed as well."

Darcy closed the catalog and put it back on the shelf. "Five-C is Buckingham Palace." She sighed. "And I am the queen."

Niko fell to one knee, placing a small white box on her lap. "Leftover berry tart, your majesty," he said. Then, laughing, he turned to Emerald and hugged her. "One day, Princess, somebody will make a dollhouse replica of this place that could end up at the Museum of the City of New York. Mark my words."

Emerald did. As far as she was concerned there was nothing to laugh about. Perhaps one day she would look back and think that 5C had been funny. But she was certain that day would not occur until she was in a place where they would last long enough for her not to be the new girl. A place where her bedroom window might look out on a backyard full of sunlight and flowers. That place, she was beginning to think, could be a place with a renewable contract. A place called Water Gap.

Stuck in Stucksville

The next morning Emerald lay in bed staring at the ceiling. She had just awakened from a dream in which she found a secret door at the back of her closet that opened to a long hallway leading to a whole new apartment full of empty rooms. She had had this dream before. Sometimes the empty apartment included a garden, sometimes marble fireplaces and long windows looking out on lawns and trees. But now she was no longer dreaming. She was gazing instead at a brown spot on the ceiling that had been growing for several days, slowly, like her worry over not having a topic for the My New York project. She reminded herself to mention the spot before it got worse, and then realized that this could lead to another visit from Mr. Montero and more unwelcome comments from Angel. If they were lucky, by the time the ceiling fell down, they would be on their way to Water Gap.

The smell of coffee was coming from the kitchen part of the Everything Room. Saturday was a busy workday for Darcy and Niko. There were catered events and big luncheons scheduled weeks in advance. At eleven-thirty, an actress friend named Patsy usually came to sit with Emerald.

Emerald found Niko hunched over the trunk-table, a theater newspaper open before him while coffee dripped from a paper filter into a glass canister. Hot cocoa began to bubble over on the stove, and Niko jumped up to turn it off. Above the sink, magnetized to the metal cabinet, a greasy clipping from Niko's high-school alumni newspaper dangled.

Lucky Niko Costos. After appearing with wife Darcy in regional theaters all over the country, he has landed a leading role in *I'll*

Take Manhattan. Broadway bound at last, with fame and fortune on the horizon, the Costos family has settled in the posh Silk Stocking district of Manhattan's Upper East Side.

Just beneath this clipping was another, only four lines, cut from a New York newspaper.

I'll Take Manhattan, starring newcomer Niko Costos and slated for a fall opening, has been canceled, due to lack of financial backing.

Darcy groaned from behind the curtain and then poked out her face. "Tell that refrigerator to quiet down," she moaned.

"Some people have chimes, some have musical alarm clocks," Niko told her, without looking up from his paper. "Not just anyone arises to the sounds of a fridge turning over . . . *varoom, varooom.*"

Not just anyone could imitate the sound of a refrigerator turning over either. Emerald couldn't help giggling.

"Thank you, thank you." Niko accepted Emerald's laughter with a nod and a smile that always made her feel as if she were the only audience he really needed. "You know why we called you Emerald, don't you?" He asked the old question.

Emerald gave the old answer. "Because I'm your jewel."

"Who laughs at my imitations." Niko winked. "A real trouper. Born in a trunk."

Emerald knew this meant she never complained about moving from place to place or sitting in the back of dark theaters while her parents rehearsed for hours on end. She leaned over the trunk-table and speared a bagel half with her fork while Niko poured out her mug of cocoa. Darcy sat up slowly. "Oh, that coffee smell," she crooned.

Emerald took her breakfast back to Cubby with Cot and settled on her bed. Instead of lifting the shade for a few moments of courtyard search, her favorite pastime, she began to dress, tugging on her tights and woolen socks against a bitter January day.

When she returned to the Everything Room, Darcy was drinking coffee while Niko made up the bed. This was in honor of Patsy Crawford. Even so, dirty and clean clothes littered the two easy chairs they'd found at a Goodwill Store, not that anyone would want to sit on them with their stuffing popping out and springs scraping the floor. Books and papers and scripts were scattered everywhere. Niko looked around disapprovingly.

"I'm no housekeeper," Darcy said. It was her usual explanation for the mess.

"Forget housekeeping," Niko complained as Emerald reached for her jacket. "How about tidying?"

"It's hard when there isn't any room."

"Excuses, excuses."

"This is temporary," Darcy reminded him. "Back in the fall we thought we would have moved to something bigger and better by now."

"Back in the fall we thought we had great jobs," Niko said. "We were supposed to be at the beginning of a winning streak. We weren't supposed to get stuck here."

"Any minute Water Gap could come through with an offer."

"But they haven't." Niko's voice was harsh.

"Stuck," Darcy cried. "Stuck in Stucksville."

"Stuck is no excuse for dust and dirty dishes and—" Niko turned to Emerald in surprise. "Where are you going?"

"The Museum of the City of New York. I'll be back before you leave. It's only five blocks away. I told you I have a project."

"What kind of project?"

"My New York. Maybe I can get an idea at the museum," she said, not mentioning that at that moment her only idea was to be as far from the sounds of her parents' familiar argument as she could get.

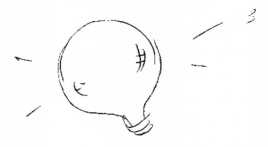

Angel's Big Idea

As she flew down the staircase, Emerald could hear the Spanish radio station through the Monteros' door. She could smell baking bread from the apartment of a man Angel called Mr. Chef. He and his wife always greeted Emerald with the words *"Buenos dias,* little one." On the floor below, where the music teacher Angel called Mrs. Piano lived, Emerald could hear someone practicing scales. Somewhere an alarm went off. A dog barked, and a baby cried.

Out on the street a sharp wind was blowing from the east, rattling the metal awning over the bodega opposite their front stoop and bending the spindly trees on the avenue. Emerald knew her way around the neighborhood, from the rows of tenements with stoops and buzzer panels to the luxury condos and co-ops with uniformed doormen and seasonal plantings of flowering shrubs and bulbs. As she sped up one street and across another, she thought how often she had passed the museum, never thinking to climb its wide marble steps.

This time, when she entered, her heart was racing. She headed quickly past the gift shop and the model of Rockefeller Center and up to the third-floor gallery of dollhouses. All to myself, she thought as she entered the dimly lit room. No Hector, no Manuel, no— A familiar figure was planted in front of the biggest case.

"Hey," Angel called out. "What are you doing here?"

"What are *you* doing here?"

"My project," Angel said.

"Me, too," Emerald answered.

"What project?"

"My project"—Emerald drew out the word— "to be here without Mrs. Alter hollering and Manny pushing and you teasing."

Angel's face seemed to collapse. "Oh," she

said, so miserably that Emerald actually believed she was sorry. "I didn't mean to tease you."

The problem with Angel was that there were two of her. The good Angel was friendly and funny and even kind. The bad Angel was tough and teasing. It was hard to know which Angel was about to happen.

"I can't believe how people lived like this." The good Angel's eyes glistened. "So nice and pretty and calm. It makes me want to get small." She giggled self-consciously. She was the biggest in the class. "And just sit down on one of those little chairs in front of that little fireplace. All beautiful and peaceful. Nothing like my house."

"Or mine," Emerald agreed.

"Yours," the bad Angel hooted. "My father says—"

"He saw our place on a bad day." Emerald cut her off.

"So show me on a good day," Angel challenged. "Invite me over right now."

"I can't. I'm busy. I have to think of a My New York project, which is pretty silly since we're just camping out in the city. We'll hear any minute about our move to Water Gap."

"Camping out?" Angel looked puzzled. "But you *live* in Five-C."

"Live in Five-C?" Emerald laughed her mother's laugh. "You mean Roach Motel? Stucksville? It's a joke."

"A *joke!*" Angel hollered. "My pop says our building is built like a fort and runs like a Swiss watch. It's where you live, and it's your New York whether you like it or not. It's no joke." She shook her head vehemently. "Where we live is important."

"Maybe for you, but not for me."

"Yes, for you, too." Angel was pink with emotion. Suddenly her expression changed from anger to excitement. "Hey," she cried, her eyes blazing so that Emerald could practically see a lightbulb going on over her head. "I'll show you where you live is important."

"Where I live is a dump," Emerald informed her. "You said yourself it's a shoe box."

"Right." Angel nodded happily. "Go get a shoe box. I'll find two and we'll put it together. Our New York. The project. Mrs. Alter said it was okay to team up. I could really *use* you."

Emerald began to back away. "I don't think so," she muttered.

"Maybe you don't"—Angel grabbed her by the arm to steer her out of the gallery and down the stairs—"but I do. My idea is so great, it's too much work for one person. Together we could win this thing."

The lightbulb had suddenly turned into a chandelier.

Montero World

One hour later, when they returned home, Emerald was carrying a book, *Decorate Your Dollhouse for a Song,* that Angel had purchased at a craft shop along with two bags full of supplies the book said she would need. To her relief, Emerald had been able to replace Angel's threatened visit with a shopping trip.

"This stuff didn't cost a song," Angel complained as they climbed the stairs to their floor. "It took all the money I made from my jobs. When you come in on the project, Emerald, you'll owe me half."

"I told you, I'm not coming in on it."

"I have to take my brothers to their sports club." Angel paused in front of her door. "I'll call you tomorrow about getting started."

"I'm not starting anything."

"Think about it," Angel called over her shoulder before closing her door.

Emerald stood in front of her own door and shook her head. It was useless telling Angel she was not on her team. Angel didn't hear what she didn't want to hear. It wasn't until Emerald was inside 5C that she realized she was still carrying *Decorate Your Dollhouse for a Song*.

Darcy sat before a large pop-up mirror, adjusting the black bow tie she wore to work at Karen's Catering. "Patsy phoned. She's got a terrible cold and can't make it. Niko's doing two shifts at Baxter's, and my job may run late." Darcy began to brush blusher all over her face. "Karen says you can come with me if you sit quiet as a mouse in the kitchen. She'll let you sample some of the goodies, too."

"Let me stay by myself," Emerald pleaded. "I won't raid the fridge the way Patsy does. I won't even charge. I'm free."

"Emerald, the jewel." Darcy laughed, tossing her blusher, brush, and mirror into a huge leather tote, which she flung over her shoulder. She scooped up her coat and drew Emerald to her for a hug. "Our self-sitting, no-cost, budget baby." She fished in her coat pocket for a piece of paper. "This is the number where I'll be. Call if you're lonesome."

"I will," Emerald promised as she watched her mother fly down the steps.

As soon as Darcy was gone, Emerald hung her jacket in the closet and carried Angel's book to her room. Cubby with Cot was just large enough to hold a bed (mattress on a platform containing three drawers), a nightstand (orange crate) with lamp on top, and a long ledge that covered the radiator and ran the length of the window. During the day this window was shaded, but toward evening, when the sky began to darken, Emerald would lift the shade to gaze across the narrow courtyard into tiers of facing windows. Each rectangle seemed to hold a small magical world inhabited by strangers. But for every one of them Emerald had a name. There was a gray-haired mustachioed man, the one Angel called

Mr. Chef, who prepared supper for himself and his wife. While he cooked, Mrs. Chef would set the table. They always dined by candlelight. An old man, the Professor, who read his paper under a yellow lamp until exactly six o'clock. A woman, Mrs. Piano, who watched as her students played their lessons and whose music filled the courtyard on warm nights when the windows were open. There was a baby, tended by his grandmother while his parents were at work, and a frail woman, the cat lady, whose cat sometimes wandered onto the fire escape and had to be coaxed back in.

Best of all was Angel's place, Montero World. Lined up like a string of bright oblongs, their spaces were so full of action that Emerald wondered how the windows could contain them. On cold nights, through steamed panes, Emerald could see Mrs. Montero chopping or stirring or sifting at her kitchen counter. Sometimes she would sit down with a cup of something to drink or visit with a neighbor or friend. Emerald could hear the laughter and the voices when the windows were open. One window down the hall looked in on little Martin, who was five, and big brother Tony. Sometimes Emerald could hear their shouts and see the pillows flying, with Mrs. Montero running from the kitchen to make peace.

But Emerald's favorite spot in Montero World was the half of a partitioned room inhabited by Angel's thirteen-year-old sister, Lenore. "She made a line down the middle," Angel had explained. "Then she put up a screen, and she said, 'If you want to visit my half, you must ask permission.'

"That's okay with me," Angel had said. "When she's not home I sneak in and try on all her clothes. Nobody knows."

But Emerald did. She had watched Angel do it.

When Lenore was alone, Emerald saw her put on makeup and take it off. Once Lenore and a girlfriend dyed their hair blue and tried to wash it out. Other times Lenore liked to pose as if she were a model in front of her long mirror, throwing out her chest and sucking in her cheeks. Sometimes she flopped on her bed to read piles of books or wrote or drew in a sketch pad. Other times she put on headphones and danced. But the most puzzling thing Lenore did was lean out on the window ledge and gaze down into the courtyard below as if she were looking for someone or something.

Though daylight viewing was risky—someone might see her—Emerald lifted her shade. The facing windows were gray and blank. After awhile she went to the Everything Room and turned on the TV. She scanned the channels—one dumb show after the other. In the fridge she found some moldy pâté from Karen's Catering. She climbed on a stool to reach for a game Grandmother Gardner had sent last Christmas, but instead pulled down a box containing Niko's cowboy boots. Emerald dumped out the boots and picked up the box, turning it this way and that.

Angel had said she lived in a shoe box. But a boot box was bigger. It was more like it. She took the empty box back to her room. *Decorate Your Dollhouse for a Song* was lying on her bed. Slowly she turned the pages. There were all sorts of ways to make simple things into dollhouse items. A wedge of cardboard from the back of her notepad stuck into the box fit exactly, creating the Everything Room and Cubby with Cot. The book suggested that empty matchboxes covered with Con-Tact paper and decorated with little knobs might work for kitchen cabinets, small tables, or trunks. Niko and Darcy collected matchboxes from all the restaurants where they had worked. They were kept in a glass bowl on top of the fridge.

Emerald brought the bowl into her room, dumped the contents on her bed, and selected some plain boxes. With a fine-tipped ballpoint pen, she carefully drew knobs and tiny drawers on their surface. Then she stuck them with glue on the wall of her boot-box Everything Room. Delighted by her efforts, she went on to paste one of Darcy's foam-rubber makeup applicators on the back of a pocket mirror to make the Murphy bed, and then she attached it to the side of the box with paper clips as the book had suggested.

At the bottom of her bed drawer, she found a box containing a family of tiny dolls, sent years before by her grandmother. They were rubbery, with bendable arms and legs wrapped in flesh-colored cloth. "Like an Ace bandage," Darcy had quipped. Emerald squeezed three dolls around the matchbox she had fashioned to look like their trunk-table. Then she stood back and smiled at the result.

Before long Niko came in the door, his face glowing from the cold. He carried a leftover shell steak with roasted baby root vegetables and potatoes. Everything was still warm in the restaurant take-out package. "What's my jewel up to?" He kissed Emerald in the doorway.

"Nothing really," she said, suddenly shy about what she had been "up to."

A few moments later, Darcy came up the stairs, holding before her a large take-out bag from Karen's Catering. "We are a microwave zap away from the gourmet event of the week," she cried. "Chicken in wine sauce, artichokes, and pilaf."

Emerald went to set the trunk while her parents debated about whether to have steak or chicken. The dishes from breakfast and the night before were still in the sink.

"I thought it was your turn to clean up," Niko accused Darcy.

She unbelted her coat, tossed it on the easy chair, and shrugged. "Forgot," she said.

Niko filled the sink with hot water and detergent.

Emerald picked up a towel.

"I'll take care of it," Niko said in a tone full of resentment.

"It's high sulk time," Darcy muttered under her breath.

Emerald headed back to Cubby with Cot. As far as she was concerned, it was storm watch time. She had learned to recognize the signs of gathering black clouds and knew how to wait out bad weather behind closed doors, doing something—reading, courtyard searching—till the coast was clear.

"Your turn, my turn," Darcy's voice was rising. "I don't care if the dishes break. Let's use paper."

Emerald put her fingers in her ears, but they were of no use. Hoping for a view of Lenore, she lifted her shade and gazed out over Niko's boot box into the windows across the courtyard and, to her dismay, into the frowning face of Angel Montero. Emerald pretended she hadn't seen Angel, but it was difficult, since Angel had begun to wave at her. There was nothing to do but wave back before pulling the shade down.

"Paper plates are expensive." Niko's tone was harsh as well as loud. "We can't afford them."

The sight of Angel reminded Emerald of her math homework. Usually she didn't look at the assignments until Sunday night, when the thought of them gave her a sinking feeling. Since she was already sunk, this might be a good time to work. With a heavy heart, she opened her math book.

When she had first arrived in Mrs. Alter's class, she knew the math from her last school. She knew it so well, she had given Angel the answers to problems. She knew it so well, she stopped paying attention until, suddenly, she was behind. What difference did it make? In another year she would be in another school where the math might be easy again. She began to look for a pencil. But the pencil was missing and her ballpoint pen was fading. She screwed it open. The little spring that held the ink shaft in place fell out onto her bed. It would be perfect for the popped-out spring of the easy chair in her model of the Everything Room. She reached for *Decorate Your Dollhouse for a Song* and was soon following instructions on how to cut a toothpaste box into the shape of a chair.

Through her closed door she heard Niko yelling, "Why don't you ever clean this place up?"

"Why don't you?" Darcy prided herself on being heard in the last row of the balcony.

"We can't invite friends. Emerald has never even had a visitor."

Darcy began to cry. "It's Stucksville."

Then the doorbell rang.

"Uh-oh," Niko gasped. "Visitors."

"Complaining neighbors." Darcy sounded frightened. "Were we yelling?"

Emerald heard the front door open. A moment later Niko poked his head in her room. "Someone to see you, Em."

On the doorstep, staring bug-eyed into the Everything Room, was Angel Montero. "You kept my book. You waved me over," she said to Emerald. "I figure you decided you want to be partners."

"Partners?" Darcy exclaimed. "How sweet."

Emerald couldn't imagine how anything could get worse, until Niko reached out a hand to draw Angel across the threshold. "We were just sitting down to dinner," he said. "Would you care to join us?"

Dining at the Ritz

"I already ate," Angel muttered, to Emerald's relief.

"Believe me, you never ate anything like artichokes in truffle oil, baby vegetables, and steak à la Baxter." Niko was clearing magazines off a chair. Darcy reached for a plate and cutlery to make a new setting.

"Thanks to the miracle of the microwave," Darcy sang, holding a platter of artichokes out for their inspection, "we can close our eyes and imagine we are dining at the Ritz."

Thanks to the miracle of Angel, Emerald thought, her parents were no longer arguing.

Darcy put an artichoke on each dish. Angel sat down. "You eat this?" she asked, poking at the green shape with her fork.

"Just watch." Niko plucked off a petal, closed his eyes, scraped the soft part of the petal off with his front teeth, and tossed what remained over his shoulder onto the floor.

Angel's jaw dropped.

Darcy burst into gales of laughter. "That's an old comedy routine from Abbott and Costello," she explained to Angel, producing a bowl for discarded leaves.

Dumbstruck, Angel nibbled suspiciously at the edge of a leaf. "Good," she finally declared.

"I told you," Darcy said, closing her eyes. "Close your eyes and you're dining at the Crème de la Ritz. Open them"—she opened them—"and you're back in the dregs of Stucksville."

"Dregs?" Angel looked puzzled. "Stucksville?"

"Our happy home." Darcy rolled her eyes to indicate the room.

Angel laid down her artichoke leaf. A blush spread up from her neck to her cheeks. "My father says this building is built like a fort," she barked, "and it runs like a Swiss watch, and we should be proud to live in such a place."

Darcy and Niko fell silent. Emerald's heart beat in her ears.

"I'll do the dishes," Darcy told Niko.

After dinner, while her parents cleared and cleaned up, Emerald drew Angel into her room.

"You are very smart to team up with me," Angel assured her, looking around for a place to sit and realizing the only spot was the bed. "You gave me math, and now I give you a project. Together we win."

"Math is different from projects," Emerald argued. "Projects are personal."

"Who says math isn't personal?" Angel snapped. "You personally used to know it and now you personally don't."

"I told you, I stopped paying attention."

"That's your whole problem," Angel began to lecture. "It's like you think you're on a fast train just passing through. But the fact is, you live here, girl. You aren't outta here yet."

Emerald couldn't decide: Was this the good Angel, the bad Angel, or just the annoying Angel? Whichever one she was, there was no point in repeating her plan for a new life in Water Gap. None of the Angels would understand.

She reached behind the shade, where she had hidden the boot box, and placed it beside Angel on the bed.

At first Angel seemed baffled. Then her face brightened. "You already began," she burst out in amazement.

Emerald shrugged. "I had nothing to do all afternoon so I made this . . . Stucksville."

Angel gave her a dark look.

"That's just what my mother calls it," she hurried to say. "But it's not a project for the contest. We're supposed to write an essay."

"I tried," Angel said miserably. "I'm a talker and I get great ideas, but every time I put them on the page they go bad. When I saw those models in the museum, I could see how they told a story without using words. We could tell a story and call it Stucksville and—and—"

"Montero World," Emerald let out before she could stop herself.

"Montero World," Angel repeated rapturously. "An essay with no words."

"Is there such a thing?"

"Why not?" Angel stood up, excited. "Since my pop is the super, we could use all the leftover stuff from the basement. You should see what he's got down there. Wood and carpet and tile." She began to pace the tiny floor. "Montero World. I need two boxes divided into six spaces. Oh, boy!" Suddenly, she frowned and moaned. "Tony and little Martin will tear it apart. Lenore will put shoes in it. Where can I work?" Her large black eyes settled on Emerald.

"There isn't much room here," Emerald quickly pointed out.

"So we stack them up. No problem. Plenty of room." Angel clapped her hands. "Stacked up. Just like real. It's gonna win. Our New York."

"It's not *my* New York, and it still isn't an essay," Emerald insisted. "It's just something I did on a boring afternoon."

"That's what you think." Angel giggled. "Now give me back my book so I can catch up." As she took the book from Emerald, she smiled smugly. "I knew you'd have good ideas," she congratulated herself. "I told everybody at school. Emerald just plays dumb. But she's really smart."

After Angel left, Emerald opened her math sheets. They weren't as hard as she'd thought they'd be. In fact she had no trouble figuring out the problems. Perhaps she could figure out a project of her own if she tried. But gazing across the courtyard, nothing came to mind. She could see Angel at her small desk, slowly turning the pages of *Decorate Your Dollhouse for a Song,* a look of deep concentration on her face. Emerald lifted her arms in a stretch, touching first one wall and then the other. It seemed Cubby with Cot had expanded— as if Angel Montero had not only come through the door but knocked down a wall while she was at it.

Sunday morning Darcy and Niko slept late. Emerald finished cutting out the easy chair from a toothpaste box she found in the wastebasket. After she assembled it, she wrapped some old printed handkerchief fabric over a powder puff and made a soft seat. Then she glued the tiny spring from her ballpoint pen to the underside of the chair. When she was done, the chair looked so real, it made her laugh out loud.

"The plan for the day," Niko announced over breakfast. "We meet up with Molly and Saul at their place and then head out for a dim sum dumpling lunch in Chinatown."

Molly and Saul were old friends from drama school who had worked in the same theater company as Darcy and Niko until good offers drew them to New York. Saul was working on a daytime soap opera called *Near to My Heart*. Molly, who designed sets, was doing an off-Broadway play. She had found time to fix up a loft space downtown. It was an Everything Room, too, just different. Really different. There were soft rugs and tall screens and low sofas and pillows and, everywhere you looked, collections of baskets. All shapes and sizes and textures in pale wheat and soft brown. "Every room needs a theme," Molly said. "These baskets gave me the color and the texture I needed to unify the space."

"A theme is a very good idea," Niko agreed. "Ours is suitcases."

"He means we're ready to leave," Darcy said.

"Don't pull out yet," Saul told them. "There may be parts for both of you in *Near to My Heart*. Call my agent and ask for an appointment." He handed Niko a card. "If you get the jobs, we'll all be working together again."

"If you get the jobs, we celebrate," Molly shouted. "Make it your place, and I'll bring the food"—she winked mischievously—"unless you're still redecorating."

"No need to decorate," Darcy said crossly. "By this time next year we'll be in Water Gap."

"The Water Gap Theater? You'd leave New York?"

"It's a good regional company, one-year renewable contracts. Along with the jobs, we'll have space and light and a place to live that you couldn't mistake for a hamster cage."

"How do you feel about moving to Water Gap?" Molly asked Emerald.

"She can't wait," Darcy answered for her.

"I'd like a backyard," Emerald added, recalling one of her favorite books, *The Secret Garden.* "Where I could plant bulbs and see how they look when they come up the next year."

While they tasted dumplings and sipped tea, Emerald decided she would plant daffodils in the backyard and maybe some tulips, with a border of pansies. She liked pansies the best. The theme of her room in Water Gap would be pansies. She would find pictures of them to hang, and perhaps even locate the wallpaper she had seen on a stage set that was covered with them. The flowers' little frowning faces wobbling on their stems always made her smile.

When dessert came, it was a platter of pineapple chunks with scoops of vanilla ice cream topped by a tiny umbrella that could open and close. Emerald eyed the umbrella, then snatched it up and tucked it into her coat pocket. She could just imagine it along with a tiny plastic broom (they did really have a broom) stuck in a thimble that looked like a miniature umbrella stand. She'd put it next to the door of the boot box. . . . Suddenly Emerald couldn't wait to get home.

Buried Treasure

Monday morning Mrs. Alter clapped her hands. "Okay, okay everybody, attention. Quiet. Today we have the citywide tests. It's time to show how smart we are at P.S. 112."

Emerald waited as the exams were distributed and the room grew still with nervous energy. It seemed no sooner had she been "smart" for one school than she was being asked to be smart for another. So far she figured she had been dumb for three different schools in three different parts of the country, like a secret agent, bringing down scores before moving on to some unsuspecting new school district. When she opened the exam she was relieved to find that she was not as dumb as she had been in her last school. With any luck, by the time she landed in Water Gap she would be brilliant.

After the time was up, everyone seemed jumpy. It was cold outside, so they had only half an hour in the yard. There were fights.

"Denise pushed me."

"I did not."

"You always get in the way."

Lisa Guzzman began to demonstrate the dance routine she would perform for her solo in the Our New York assembly program. A small crowd gathered. Emerald usually avoided her classmates. Especially Lisa, who talked about her dancing classes and drama classes and sounded more like Darcy or Niko than a fourth grader. But today, even in her bulky jacket and sneakers, Lisa looked so graceful and pretty that Emerald found herself joining the circle to watch her dance.

"What are you looking at?" Denise taunted. "You want to learn how to dance? Watch me!" She leaped around imitating Lisa. "Come on,

Outta-Here Emerald." Denise pulled at her sleeve. "Let's dance."

"Lay off her." Angel bore down suddenly, towering over Denise. "She's my partner."

"Your partner?" Denise repeated, puzzled. "You mean like in some kind of a business?"

"If we are, it's none of yours." Angel drew Emerald away. She took a paper bag from her knapsack. "Look," she ordered Emerald, opening the bag slowly for effect. Inside were six stuffed dolls. "Monteros for Montero World."

"But they're huge," Emerald pointed out.

"So are we," Angel agreed. "Everybody says we Monteros have big mouths and big fat heads. We fill a room twice as much as normal people." She jammed the bag back into her knapsack. "You come to my place after school and we'll hunt buried treasure."

"Buried treasure?" Emerald wasn't sure she'd heard right.

Angel lowered her head and her voice. "When people move out of the building, you wouldn't believe what they leave behind. Some of it we send off to Goodwill, but some of it is in my pop's basement."

"Buried treasure," Emerald repeated. The junk that got left behind in Stucksville. Darcy would laugh out loud.

But a few hours later, when Angel led Emerald down the long basement corridor, Emerald began to wonder.

After the noise and bustle of the Monteros' apartment, the humming, buzzing, and clicking of the boilers, meters, and pipes that kept the building warm and bright seemed as soothing as ocean waves breaking on a beach.

"My pop knows every sound," Angel boasted. "He can tell if anything is broken just by listening. He says this building is built like a fort and—"

"Runs like a Swiss watch," Emerald interrupted.

"That's right." Angel nodded happily, as if Emerald were a good student who had finally learned a lesson. She took her by the hand and led her past Mr. Montero's office, a small room containing an old desk heaped with papers and tools and bits of hardware. Behind the desk was a pegboard, where more tools and cables were hung. They passed walls covered with meters behind glass till they reached a door marked PRIVATE. Angel pushed it open.

Behind this door was a large cool room packed

with things that had been left behind. There were mounds of carpet remnants and rolled-up rugs and linoleum sheets. There were stacks of tile and squares of wood flooring. There were old-fashioned lamps and chairs and sofas piled atop one another. There was a corner filled with cartons containing glasses and china plates and photographs and even some paintings in frames.

"Look." Angel pointed out a pile of small rugs and carpet pieces. "We could use some of these."

Emerald spotted a square of carpet that she could cut to fit Stucksville. Just below it was a fringed rug, covered with blue flowers. She could imagine it beside her bed, something to put between her bare feet and the floor on a freezing morning.

"Take it," Angel said, reading her mind. "It would look great next to your bed."

Angel helped herself to some rolls of wallpaper and curtain material that was buried under a pile of table mats. In the corner of a deep carton, Emerald caught sight of a blue vase. It was the same blue as her new rug.

"Here." Angel handed her the vase and scooped up a few dusty silk flowers next to it.

"Pansies," Emerald marveled.

By the time they were ready to go upstairs, their arms were full.

On the first floor Mrs. Lauffer was returning with bags of groceries. "Someone's decorating." She smiled knowingly as she passed them on the steps.

On the second floor Mrs. Chef was going out to walk her dog. "What's happening?" she asked. "Moving day?"

"Sort of," Angel said.

Emerald hoped she wasn't carrying something Mrs. Chef had thrown out.

On the third floor, the sounds of music wafted from under Mrs. Piano's door and the smell of baking bread drifted from the Chefs' apartment. Grandma Diaz was putting out garbage. "Anything for me?" she cackled. Little Toby watched them from behind her skirt.

Angel greeted each person they met by name. "Hello, Mr. Ortiz"—Mr. Chef's real name. "Hi, Mrs. Lauffer." *"Buenos dias,* Mrs. Diaz."

"You know everybody," Emerald said.

Angel nodded. "I know all about them, too. I mean, I know when Mrs. Farmer's had too much to drink and when Mr. and Mrs. Ortiz have an argument. When my sister, Lenore, used to have a crush on Lenny Lauffer and hang around the first-floor mailboxes all the time waiting for him till my mom told her to cut it out, I knew he didn't know she was alive."

"The walls are pretty thin," Emerald said, remembering Darcy and Niko's argument and how Angel had rung their bell right in the middle of it.

"Yes," Angel agreed, without thinking. "I hear a lot." Then she clapped her hand over her mouth and turned red. "But I never listen. I get to know stuff because I stay put. Not like somebody who moves around all the time."

"My parents go where there's work. They're actors."

"Actors!" Angel cried. "I knew it. I told everybody. I said Emerald is smart but she plays dumb, and her parents are beautiful like movie stars. They could end up rich and famous, and I would be the one who gets invited to visit them in Hollywood." They were climbing the last flight and Angel was huffing and puffing with effort and excitement.

"Is that why you picked me to be your partner?"

"Partly." Angel nodded. When Emerald frowned

and didn't say anything, she burst out laughing. "Well, did you think it was because of your huge apartment?"

Then Emerald had to laugh, too.

Darcy was sitting on the Murphy bed reading a script. "There's some leftover berry tart in the fridge." She waved at the kitchen wall without lifting her eyes from the page. "I think we're out of milk." On the cover binder of Darcy's script, in bold letters, was written *Near to My Heart*.

Angel sucked in her breath, and her eyes glowed. "My sister, Lenore, used to watch that show every chance she got, till my mother said it made her boy crazy and she had to stop. Now Lenore's thirteen. She's not boy crazy, she's clothes crazy. She wants to be a designer. No more time for the soaps."

"I wish I'd watched with your sister Lenore," Darcy said, not looking up from the script. "I'm auditioning for the show on Monday, and I can't keep track of this plot."

Emerald pulled Angel into Cubby with Cot, eager to unload their buried treasure, which Darcy had been too preoccupied to even notice.

The little flowered rug was perfect beside

Emerald's bed. The blue vase on top of her radiator made a pool of light that reminded her of a calm lake with pansy faces wobbling comically at the shore. Angel took *Decorate Your Dollhouse for a Song* from her knapsack and dumped out all her supplies so that every inch of the bed was covered.

"I'm just helping you," Emerald reminded her. "I'm not joining you."

"That's too bad." Angel shook her head sadly. "You're good at this. You have small fingers."

Whether it was small fingers or some kind of talent, Emerald knew Angel was right. She was good at measuring and cutting and drawing tiny knobs. She was good at fashioning small items out of clay. She showed Angel how to cut paper for her kitchen, and how to make tables out of pocket mirrors and spools, and bookcases from matchboxes. After a while Angel looked at her watch.

"I've got to go to my job now," she said importantly. "I walk the piano teacher's dog, Millie, on Mondays, Tuesdays, and Thursdays. Also I pick up the mail for Mrs. Farmer when she's feeling . . . low. I do her grocery shopping and buy food for

Oz, the cat. I water Mr. and Mrs. Ortiz's plants when they go on vacation, and I feed the Diazes' cat when Grandma doesn't come and the family is away."

"How did you get those jobs?"

Angel zipped up her jacket. "Like I told you, everybody knows I'm around. They can count on me."

When she was gone, Emerald cleared all the paper and scraps off her bed and tucked the boxes on the window ledge behind her shade. In the Everything Room Darcy had put away her script and was watching her favorite old movie channel.

"Rear Window," Darcy told Emerald. "It's about a man who solves a murder mystery by noticing the goings-on in an apartment across the way from his."

Emerald returned to her room and lifted the shade. She was far more interested in watching the apartments across from hers than in seeing a movie about a man who watched the apartment across from his, even if he solved a murder. No movie could match Lenore Montero dancing freestyle around her room with a headset on, or

Angel's brothers having one of their fights over little Martin's favorite superhero doll, pulling it this way and that until Tony managed to grab the toy from his brother and toss it into the corner. When, to Emerald's delight, Martin retrieved the doll, Tony wrenched it out of his hands again, this time waving it above his head in a teasing way, until Martin, in tears, ran to fetch Mrs. Montero. The instant little Martin was out of the room, Emerald saw Tony tuck the doll under his shirt and look around for a better place to hide it. In the kitchen Mrs. Montero stopped her ironing to console Martin, while Tony circled his room, glancing this way and that until his eyes came to rest on the window. For a moment, Emerald feared he could tell she was watching, but she couldn't tear herself from the spot. Especially when she saw Tony lift the window a crack and slip the doll onto the sill. As his mother burst into the room with a wailing Martin at her side, Tony closed the window. The doll tumbled into the courtyard.

Martin's shrieks could be heard right through the glass. Mrs. Montero seemed to be hollering as well. But Tony simply shook his head and

shrugged his shoulders in an exaggerated inno-
cent way.

It was hard to watch and harder to listen to
Martin. What should she do? She knew what had
happened. She could put an end to little Martin's
misery. She had it in her power to put an end to
the scene. But would that get Tony in trouble?

"Waaaa waaaa." Emerald could hear the shrieks.

She turned away from the window. What did
she care? What business was it of hers what happened to Martin and Tony Montero?

"Waaa waaa."

Emerald took another look. Tony was still pre-
tending he had nothing to do with his brother's
misery. She didn't like the way he teased and
taunted. She folded her arms on her chest. Why
didn't she just stop watching, if she didn't like it?
Why didn't she just draw her shade? Martin
buried his miserable face in his pillow and shook
with sobs.

It was too much. Emerald reached for the cordless phone and dialed. "The superhero doll is in
the courtyard," she told Mrs. Montero quickly,
leaving it to someone else to figure out how it
got there.

Back at her window, with her heart racing, she was afraid to even show her face, let alone lean out. But soon there were voices below.

"Where?"

"Here. It's here, just like the phone said."

This was followed by a whoop of joy (Martin), scolding (Mrs. Montero), and whining denial (Tony). "I didn't do it. I don't know how it could've happened. It's like magic."

Emerald fell back on her bed and hugged her knees. Maybe she hadn't solved a murder, like the man in *Rear Window,* or watered plants, fed cats, picked up mail and groceries, and walked Millie the dog, like Angel, but helping to find little Martin's favorite toy had been the best time she could think of. She wished she could do it all over again. Solving cases. It could be her job. She had been lucky to have Angel's phone number to make the call. All she needed now was a sharp eye and more phone numbers, and she would be all set.

Rear Window

"**S**omebody called my house yesterday and told my mother that Tony threw Martin's superhero doll out the window," Angel announced on the way to school. "Martin thinks it was the FBI or the CIA."

The FBI or the CIA? Emerald nearly laughed out loud. It was all she could do to keep from saying that she had been the one.

"Whoever it was better watch out," Angel went on. "Tony says if he finds out, he'll beat them to tapioca pudding."

But he wasn't going to find out. Not if she

could help it. This was secret work. Better done alone. Anyway, who wanted to get beaten to tapioca pudding?

In school Mrs. Alter took them to the library on the fourth floor. They were supposed to learn how to find a book.

"If you know the alphabet, you can look it up," Mrs. Alter said.

Of course! Emerald realized. She could take the names of the tenants in her building off the mailbox listings in the downstairs hallway and look them up in the telephone directory. She didn't need to ask Angel and arouse suspicion. Scanning the shelves, she was amazed to see a copy of *Decorate Your Dollhouse for a Song* in the nonfiction section. She took the book to the librarian's desk and signed it out. If she changed her mind about the project, she wouldn't need to borrow Angel's book either.

As soon as school was out, Angel hurried after Emerald. "Six lollipop sticks for curtain rods. I had to eat through a whole box." She stuck out her purple tongue as proof. "Grape," she said. "You should see what other great stuff I've got."

The other great stuff was dumped out on

Emerald's bed as soon as they entered her room. There was Con-Tact paper that looked like wood and corrugated cardboard to use for books on the bookshelf.

They cut the cardboard into strips and then, with a fine brush, carefully painted each ripple of paper a different color to look like a row of book spines on a shelf. By the time they were done, Angel had to walk Mrs. Piano's dog, Millie.

"Come with me," she suggested.

Emerald placed their models on the window ledge. She was glad Angel had asked.

On Mrs. Piano's floor she heard the sound of a small dog yapping as well as piano scales. When Angel rang the bell, the piano stopped, but the barking got louder and louder until the door opened a crack and a wild ball of white fur whizzed past Mrs. Piano's ankles and into Emerald's shins, where it came to a startled stop.

"Hello, New Girl in the Building," Mrs. Piano greeted Emerald. "And Angel, you are just in time." She beckoned to them both. "You will hear some Mozart. My student would rather be doing something else. Maybe an audience will help him play with more enthusiasm."

They followed Mrs. Piano's round figure down the dark corridor, over a carpet patterned like the floor of an enchanted forest, into a room filled with plants, floor to ceiling bookshelves, and a grand piano. Mrs. Piano ordered them to sit on a small velvet sofa opposite her shy student. He was none other than Guthry Lauffer, and, from the look of him, an audience was not going to help him play with more enthusiasm.

"Guthry will now perform," Mrs. Piano commanded. "From beginning to end. No stops."

Pale as a paper towel, with his eyes glued to the notes, Guthry played so fast that beginning to end was over with no apparent middle.

"Where's the fire?" Mrs. Piano cried. She attached a leash to Millie's collar and handed it to Angel. "I am Madame Wyzinski." She put out her hand to Emerald. "I have been observing your interesting boxes on the window ledge."

"It's our project for the My New York essay contest," Angel boasted. "We're teammates."

"Teammates?" Emerald said "Remember, I told you before, I'm just helping you, not joining you."

"I don't have a topic yet," Guthry confessed. "I can't think of one."

"Neither could she." Angel pointed to Emerald. "She's lucky I decided to include her in mine. She's doing Five-C, and I'm doing A."

Emerald glared at Angel, who was not listening.

"I thought the project was an essay," Guthry said, puzzled. "Two pages long."

"This is an essay without words," Angel assured him.

"Is there such a thing?"

"No, there isn't," Emerald snapped. "And I am not her teammate."

"Then you are a complete loser," Angel spat out. "And you won't have anything to show." She yanked on Millie's leash and set off down the long corridor, pulling the little dog behind her.

Guthry hurried in Angel's footsteps. "I wonder . . . if I did my place, could I be in on it, too?"

"No way," Angel replied over her shoulder. "I have enough trouble with the partner I've got."

Before Emerald could protest once again that she was *not* a partner, Angel flew down the stairs after Millie. Mrs. Piano stood in her open doorway waiting for her next pupil. She put a hand on Guthry's shoulder. "Perhaps," she said gently, "if you doodled less, you would have more time to practice the piano and find ideas for homework projects on your own."

Guthry stared at his feet as Mrs. Piano closed the door. "I love to draw," he told Emerald apologetically. "Someday I want to make comics for the papers. My brother says I'm good." Guthry raised his blue-green eyes to Emerald's face and smiled. Like his brother, Lenny, he had a great smile. Suddenly Emerald felt happy and dreamy all at once. Now, for the first time, she understood why Lenore once acted so silly about Guthry's brother.

"Do you really want to be in on Angel's project?" she asked.

Guthry nodded. "I can't write an essay. I tried. If it's not a comic strip, I can't think of anything."

"Okay." Emerald let out a sigh. "I'll get you in on it."

"But you said you weren't—"

She shook her head. "I changed my mind."

Emerald accompanied Guthry down to his floor and waited until he had gone into his apartment. Then she copied the names of each tenant from the mailboxes.

Upstairs in 5C, she went through the telephone

directory and made up a neat list of numbers in the back of her notebook. There was a number for each window she observed. When she got to Guthry's, she switched to her new purple-ink pen, writing carefully and then underlining the number with three strong lines.

Maybe Angel knew the names of everybody in the building, and even got jobs because the tenants could count on her. Maybe she knew inside stuff, like when Mr. and Mrs. Chef had an argument or when Mrs. Farmer had too much to drink. But now, thanks to her window, she, Emerald, was going to know things, too. Things that even Know-It-All Angel had no idea about.

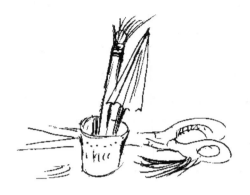

Emerald to the Rescue

"You changed your mind about being partners," Angel crowed. "I knew it. I knew you would."

"There's a but."

"What's the but?"

"If I'm in, so is Guthry."

"Guthry?" Angel bellowed. "He'll do something stupid and ruin everything."

"He's an artist," Emerald said. "He'll make great stuff."

"Oh, sure, like the picture of Mrs. Alter he drew on the board before she came in the room and then had to go to the principal to explain."

Angel thought for a moment. "His mother, she grew up in the building. She and her husband work out of the apartment. Designs by Lauffer, Inc. They design things like ads and boxes. They knocked down some walls and made a big room like a studio out of it. My pop was afraid the whole building would collapse. He had to call in the Department of Buildings and couldn't sleep for a week."

"You know so much about everybody," Emerald said, thinking this was a good time to gather information. "What about the man you call the Professor?"

"Dr. Hahn? We call him the Professor because he taught in a college in South America till he had to leave because they changed the government. The Lauffers do his shopping and look in on him. That's why they have his key."

"What about Mr. Ortiz?" Emerald asked, pulling Angel further away from the subject of Guthry Lauffer joining the team. "You always call him Mr. Chef because he does the cooking."

"He *is* a chef." Angel took a deep breath. "He cooks at the Waldorf-Astoria hotel. He's got autographs all over his walls. Presidents and movie stars. Mrs. Farmer, she was a bookkeeper, she loves her cat. Sometimes when she's feeling low, I buy her groceries." Angel was on a roll. "Nobody can pronounce the piano teacher's name. We call her Mrs. Piano. She was very rich once upon a time back in Europe."

"Who else can you tell me about?" Emerald said.

"There's *us*," Angel cried. "The Monteros. Tony calls us the First Family of the building because my pop, he makes it run, like the president. If there's a neighbor who's got a problem, you call Montero."

"That's why I knew you would let Guthry in on the project," Emerald crowed triumphantly. "He's a neighbor, and he's got a problem."

For a moment Angel's jaw actually fell open. She had walked into a trap, and the lid had slammed shut. "Okay," she said with a heavy sigh. "I'll tell him he's in."

"You're in," Angel called over to Guthry's desk the following morning in school.

"You won't be sorry," he shouted back.

After the last bell he was waiting for them on

the sidewalk outside. "I already started," he reported. His face was red, his eyes intense. "My model will be awesome. You'll see."

On the frozen walk home none of them spoke. But just before opening his door Guthry paused and cleared his throat. "You won't believe this."

What Emerald couldn't believe was what the Lauffers had done to their apartment. It was hard to imagine that they lived in the same building. Everything had been scooped out, rooms joined together and moldings removed, to form large, neat, oblong-shaped spaces in which there were a few simple pieces of furniture, including drawing boards, light boxes, files, and computers. Mr. and Mrs. Lauffer and Guthry's brother were all at work in different parts of the room.

"Hello, Guth," Mrs. Lauffer called out. When she noticed Angel and Emerald, she added, "And guests."

"Help yourself from the tray." Mr. Lauffer tipped his head toward a tray with a pitcher of juice, crackers, glasses, and fruit.

"No, thank you," Angel said primly, frowning at the food as if it were as peculiar as the floor plan and should also be looked into by a city inspector.

"This is mine." Guthry pointed proudly to the stand on which a thin wooden box lay open on one side. Inside the crate he had already begun to assemble models of the Lauffers' furniture, made of large paper clips and scraps of cloth.

"How did you do this?" Angel asked, amazed. "You don't have the book."

"I have this." Guthry tapped his forehead. "Where do you think my pictures come from?"

"We didn't help him, if that's what you're thinking," Lenny said, turning from his drawing board.

With his face framed by the courtyard outside and a pale light falling on his cheek, Emerald could certainly understand why Lenore had a crush on him. She went over to the Lauffers' window and looked up toward Angel's place. There was Lenore staring down as Emerald had seen her do so often before. But now she knew why.

"We better get to work," Angel said, tugging Emerald's sleeve, "or he'll be done before we are."

Back in Cubby with Cot, they selected small pictures from magazines to paste into round buttons and glue onto the walls of Montero World. "Just like the paintings in our living room," Angel marveled. They made mirrors by folding aluminum foil around squares of cardboard and tacking them up with small pins. After the pictures and the mirrors were hung and the corrugated cardboard glued into matchboxes to resemble books on a bookshelf, Angel and Emerald stood back to admire their work.

"How do we get them to school?" Angel wondered.

"Shopping bags," Emerald suggested, producing two from Karen's Catering.

"People will think Our New York is food," Angel worried. "What will they say when they see what's inside?"

"It won't be long before we find out." Emerald glanced at the calendar that hung over the top of her cot. "A week from Friday."

"I wish it would go on longer," Angel said. "I wish we could do the whole building. That's what I wish."

And what about the courtyard? Emerald thought. She could draw the windows of her view onto a piece of oaktag and make a fire escape out of tongue depressors. On the fire escape she could put some of the little plastic animals she had once collected. There was a cat and a dog. "It's good Guthry came in on the project," she said. "We can do more of the building."

"Guthry's not so bad," Angel conceded, unaware of Emerald's glance into the courtyard. "It just made me mad that Lenny never paid attention to Lenore. I'm glad she doesn't think about him anymore."

That's what *you* think! Emerald thought. Perhaps in her drawing of Lenore's window she would actually show her with her nose pressed to the pane.

After seeing Guthry's model, Emerald's mind raced. She had never made the broom that would sit beside the tiny umbrella in the thimble umbrella stand. What could she fashion it from? The book had said a paintbrush would work, but she only had one paintbrush, and she needed it. Be creative, she thought. Try something that's not in the book. Guthry didn't follow a book.

As soon as Angel was gone, she examined her paintbrush. What was it but a stick with some brown hairs at the end? All she needed was a stick; the brown hairs were growing on her head. She located a toothpick in the kitchen Everything Drawer and snipped enough hair from a spot at the top of her head to fit out a tiny broom. But the end of the toothpick was too small and the hairs had nothing to stick to. Perhaps one of Angel's lollipop sticks would work better if it were cut in half. She snipped another clump of hair off the top of her head and this time wrapped one end in masking tape before attaching it to the stick. Too thin, Emerald decided. Finally it was a pencil stub that looked best. She stood it upright in the thimble beside her Chinese umbrella, where it seemed to her a good replica of the original. In fact, the little collection of things in the thimble struck Emerald as so funny, she could hardly stop gazing at it. She couldn't wait to hear what Guthry would say.

After a while the light began to grow dim. It was time to tidy up the bits and scraps of material and lift her shade for a study of the courtyard. Before long the Professor turned off his lamp, just as Darcy turned on the news. Lenore and a girlfriend were trying on scarves. Mr. and Mrs. Chef were preparing dinner. Mrs. Piano was teaching a lesson. Baby Diaz was crawling on a floor packed with toys while his grandmother watched television. Grandma Diaz checked her watch and got up to go to the kitchen. Baby Diaz lifted the edge of the bed skirt and rolled his truck right under the bed, following after with his head and his arms and legs until he had completely disappeared. After a moment the truck appeared on the other side of the bed with Baby Diaz right behind it. To his delight, the baby seemed to have discovered a new game. Immediately he rolled the truck back under the bed, following it until he was gone from view. Only this time Emerald was alarmed to see that he did not crawl out on the other side. When Grandma Diaz returned to the bedroom she looked about her and called out playfully as if it were a game. But very quickly, she grew worried. Emerald watched as she scurried from window to window, checking metal guards and even glancing into the courtyard. She became more frantic by the moment, opening the closets and cupboards, craning her head this way and that, searching every corner. Emerald's heart beat fast. She held her breath. It was as if Grandma Diaz's distress was catching. "Look under the bed," Emerald said out loud, over and over. Finally, she reached for the list of neighbors' numbers and dialed. "He's under the bed," she said quickly, before hanging up. Then she peered out the window to watch as Grandma Diaz got down on her knees, lifted the bed skirt, and gently slid the sleeping baby and his truck out onto the carpet.

Emerald jumped up from her bed, hugging herself and laughing out loud. She felt like one of the sprites she had read about in fairy-tale books, entering people's lives to offer help, surprise, and pleasure. Grandma Diaz sat in the rocking chair with the baby on her lap. Soon they were both asleep.

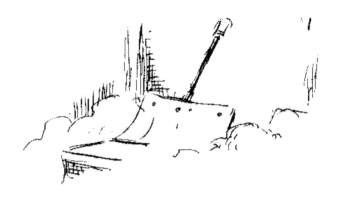

Blizzard Brigade

Saturday morning Patsy Crawford called to say she was still sick.

"I sat myself last week," Emerald reminded Darcy. "Please let me do it again."

"It looks like snow," Darcy answered, glancing nervously at the weather report on the television screen. "There's no food in the house, and I am nervous out of my skull over Monday's auditions. Two of them. *Near to My Heart* and Water Gap on the same day. I don't need something else to fret over. We'll take heaps of books and puzzles, and I'll stuff you with foie gras and caviar blinis. It won't be so bad."

"Yes, it will," Emerald insisted. "I want to go to Angel's."

"Were you invited?"

"Lots of times," she fibbed.

On the telephone Mrs. Montero assured Darcy that Emerald was very welcome and "should come right away. We keep an eye on your baby," she promised.

As Darcy put on her coat, she paused and glanced back at Emerald. "Good grief!" she gasped, narrowing her eyes and clapping a hand over her mouth. "Is that a new style, or has some creature been chewing at the top of your head?"

Emerald reached up to touch her spiky hair. "I got some glue on it that wouldn't comb out."

"Never mind." Darcy patted the cropped spot. "It will grow back." She wound a scarf around her neck. "I just wish it would snow already."

And then it did!

By the time Emerald arrived at Angel's, the flakes had begun to fall and the Montero kitchen was turning into a blizzard control center. Emerald never dreamed what a snowstorm meant in the life of a building super. There was the oil to check. There were pipes to worry about. Bags of salt had to be hauled up from the basement to be scattered on the stoop and the sidewalk, which would have to be shoveled later. Up and down the stairs Angel, Lenore, Tony, and Emerald trudged. It wasn't long before Guthry opened his door armed with a brand-new orange shovel. "Call me when it's shovel time," he said.

Angel laughed. "You want in on this project, too?"

By midmorning the sky was white with soft-falling thick snow. Traffic noises were muffled. Only a few cars and buses crept up Madison Avenue.

Angel banged on Guthry's door. "You're on," she hollered.

They started at the front door, clearing each step of the stoop. Then they moved to the side-walk, mounding heaps of heavy snow on the curb in larger and larger hills. As they pitched snow from sidewalk to curb, they stopped from time to time to throw back their heads, open their mouths, and catch flakes on their tongues, finally scooping up handfuls to lick and swallow.

"Have you ever tasted sugar and snow?"

Guthry asked, rubbing his stomach and licking his lips. "Delicious."

Suddenly they were hungry for more than snow.

Upstairs, Mrs. Montero had prepared a soup that was full of vegetables and beans, spicy hot, carrying warmth to the soles of their feet.

"It's a big one," Mrs. Montero said, looking out at the storm. "A real blizzard." The telephone began to ring. Mrs. Farmer wanted to know if Angel could pick up coffee and rolls for her. Mrs. Diaz was worried that there wasn't enough heating oil. Mrs. Riley's son called to say he was concerned that a window might have been left open in his mother's apartment before she went to the nursing home. Would someone check? Mrs. Montero hung up, muttering, "Who has time to look in somebody's closed apartment?" She opened a metal box marked KEYS and began to search among them.

Angel jumped up from the table. "We'll do it, Momma."

"Mmmmmm." Mrs. Montero considered.

"We won't touch anything, and we'll lock up good. I promise. Me and Emerald."

The phone rang again, and Mrs. Montero handed her the keys. "Be careful you don't break anything," she warned.

From the moment Angel opened the door into 5D, Emerald had an eerie sense that she had entered this place before. How many times had she unlocked a secret door in her dreams that led from Cubby with Cot into unknown spaces? Now here it was. Five-D. The long corridor took off where 5C's short one ended. On either side were small dark rooms similar to Emerald's, but full of books and soft chairs on which to sit and think. At the end of the corridor a large front parlor contained a sofa, easy chairs, a sideboard full of patterned plates, and a window that overlooked the street and a beautiful snow-covered tree.

Angel checked all the windows, pushing them down for good measure and running her finger along the ledges, feeling for damp. The apartment seemed to be waiting for something. It was as still as an empty stage. "Sometimes when people move out and leave stuff, we have to call Goodwill to cart away what we can't sell or store or use," Angel said, looking around like a shopper. "I wonder what Mrs. Riley will do." She closed the door carefully behind her and locked it double.

Back in the Monteros' kitchen they returned the key to its box and put on their stiff dried gloves and jackets. "Shovel brigade," Angel called, leading the way downstairs and even remembering to bang on Guthry's door.

The snow was falling so fast, it was up to their knees. They heaped it as best as they could onto the great curbside mounds. Guthry made a tunnel in one of the mounds and crawled inside. Emerald followed after. "This is nice," she complimented him. "Like an igloo."

"I'm good at making things," Guthry agreed. "Lenny likes my model so much he started one of his own for his high school project in architecture. Tomorrow I'm taking him to see the houses we saw on that museum class trip."

"What time?" Emerald asked.

"Around noon," Guthry said. "How come?"

"No reason." She tried to sound cool, though she could scarcely contain herself. "Maybe Angel and I ought to take another look, too."

"Another look at what?" Angel hollered into the

tunnel, edging her way through on hands and knees. "I'm listening."

"It's not big enough for three," Guthry warned, too late. The top of the tunnel began to cave in on them, and they were in snow up to their necks. It seemed the only thing to do was roll in it, make balls of it, and throw the balls at one another before climbing out on top, breathless with laughter.

There were no longer any cars on the street. Only an occasional bus crawled up Madison Avenue, its lights looking magical and soft through the snowy sky. In the blue-gray light, Emerald could see Darcy and Niko carrying groceries and picking their way, like a pair of phantoms in a dream. To Emerald, the whole day had been a dream.

Up in Cubby with Cot, listening to her parents rehearsing their lines while preparing dinner in the Everything Room, she reached for the cordless phone and dialed Angel's number, watching through the window as Lenore picked up her ringing portable.

"Tomorrow at noon," Emerald hissed. "The Museum of the City of New York. Be there! Take

Angel and Emerald, and you will meet the boy of your dreams."

She hung up, breathless with excitement and delight, her pulse throbbing in her head. What had she done?

Matchmaker?

Sunday morning brilliant sunlight penetrated into the courtyard, where glistening mounds of snow decorated every window ledge and icicles hung from the gutters. Darcy and Niko were rehearsing again for their auditions on Monday.

"Please answer all phone calls," Darcy shouted to Emerald just as the telephone began to ring. "We cannot be disturbed."

"You won't believe this," Angel announced into Emerald's ear. "Lenore wants to take me to the museum to check out the model houses. She says she needs a few decorating ideas for her room."

"Anything else?" Emerald asked.

"Yes, you can come, too. We leave at noon."

Emerald opened her notebook to the last page. Under the word *Cases* she wrote *1. Superhero Locator. 2. Baby Finder.* Then she paused for a moment before writing the last entry: *3. Matchmaker?*

Amazingly, by late morning the snow of yesterday had turned to black slush, and rivers of water rushed into drains or collected in pools. Angel and Lenore tried to leap over them, while Emerald, in Darcy's rubber boots, waded straight through.

As they climbed the marble museum stairs, Lenore took out her sketch pad and a pencil. "I'm ready," she said.

Entering the grand foyer, Angel let out a shout.

There was Guthry, standing with Lenny before a model of Rockefeller Center.

"My brother wanted to check out the models," Guthry told her. "What are you doing here?"

"My sister—" Angel stopped speaking. A deep blush rose from her neck as she glanced over to Lenore. "She wanted to check out the models, too."

"I'm looking for decorating ideas," Lenore said quickly, waving her sketch pad in the air as proof.

"We all have a right to be here," Lenny said, smiling. "We live in this town, and this is our museum. It belongs to us."

"So when do we move in?" Guthry asked.

"Very funny," Lenny said, as if it wasn't. "As a matter of fact, I wouldn't mind living in this place."

"Me, neither," Lenore agreed. She was nodding so hard, she looked like a toy dog in the rear window of a car.

"I would," Angel disagreed. "I mean, if you got up in the night and wanted something to eat, it could take till morning to find the kitchen. You wouldn't know the neighbors. It would be lonely."

As they began to climb the staircase Emerald thought about living in the mansion. Angel was right. It would be lonely. She would miss the smell of bread baking and the sound of a dog barking. She would really miss looking out her window into all the bright worlds across the courtyard.

On the stairway they passed a group of students speaking in French. Another guided tour stood before a portrait of George Washington, listening to their leader discuss the portrait in

Japanese. "People say New Yorkers take their city for granted," Lenny told Lenore, "and it's the visitors who really appreciate it."

"They're wrong," Angel disagreed. "Me and you and Lenore and Guthry are native New Yorkers, and we don't take it for granted. Emerald was born somewhere else, and she can't wait to leave."

"Is that true?" Guthry asked in surprise.

"She's outta here in a year," Angel answered, as if she was proud of knowing something about Emerald that Guthry didn't.

The others looked at Emerald in disbelief, waiting for her to agree or argue. "Let's go to the dollhouse floor," was all she could manage to say.

They fell silent as they entered the third-floor gallery of house models. The darkened room and small, spotlit cases glowed like jewels. Lenore took out her pad and began to draw. Lenny opened his notebook to sketch.

"Hey," Guthry nudged Emerald. "Look what we started."

"We?" Angel barked.

"You," Emerald acknowledged. "It was all your idea."

"That's right." Angel accepted the compliment, thinking it had to do with models, not matchmaking. Matchmaking Lenore and Lenny was not on her list of jobs. "But you each helped. We are a good team."

"The Designing Dynamos." Guthry held up both thumbs.

Lenny looked over Lenore's shoulder at her sketch. "Apply to Art and Design," he advised, "and you'll learn how to get started in a career."

Lenore beamed. "This drawing will go into my portfolio."

"If you ever want to visit the school, I'd be happy to show you around," Lenny told her. "I'm in my second year."

"Thanks." Lenore blushed. "I had no idea."

Emerald felt Angel's elbow in her ribs. "No idea? Ha!"

Back on her bed in Cubby with Cot, Emerald took out her notebook and erased the question mark after *Matchmaker.*

What's in the Bag?

Niko and Darcy weren't home yet when Emerald and Angel returned from school on Monday. "They're still auditioning," Emerald said, taking off her jacket and hanging it along with Angel's on a door hook. She cleared her bed in order to set up their work. First they sorted lollipop sticks for curtain rods and cut another toothpaste box for the frame of a chair. They measured Con-Tact paper to cover the floors and made squares out of old washcloths for scatter rugs. A few powder puffs covered in fabric became throw pillows to place on the Montero sofa. Emerald scooped some soft stuffing out of an easy chair and scattered it on the floor of her model. Then, for good measure, she fished a dust ball out from under the chair and placed it in the corner of the box.

"What are you doing?" Angel asked.

"Making it more like home," Emerald said, laughing.

"Stuffing and dust balls all over the floor are funny?"

"It's what my parents call an inside joke," Emerald explained.

Angel shook her head disapprovingly and glanced at her watch. "Time to walk Millie," she announced, dusting bits of fabric from her lap. At the door she was met by Darcy and Niko, fishing for their keys.

"Two auditions in one day." Niko collapsed on one of the easy chairs, while Darcy sank into the pile of clothes on the other. "Ouch," she winced. "These things get flatter by the minute." Then she smiled. "We were really good. They liked us but won't let us know if we got the jobs till later."

"'Tomorrow, tomorrow.'" Niko gave Emerald a hug along with his rendition of the song from *Annie.* "Wish us luck for tomorrow."

"I have a charm," Angel told them. "If I put it under my pillow and make a wish, sometimes I get my wish. I'll make my wish for you to have good luck tomorrow."

"Then we can't fail," Niko said, laughing. "What have you two been up to in that cubbyhole?"

"You don't know?" Angel exploded. "It's our project—My New York." She put her hand on Emerald's shoulder. "We're teammates. Me and Emerald and Guthry. We're making the places where we live. Just like at the museum."

"Can we see?" Darcy asked.

There was no way to say no. As she helped Angel bring their boxes into the room Emerald was half-tempted to drop hers on the floor and hope for its temporary destruction.

"Oh, my!" Darcy exclaimed, going pale under her makeup. "Just look at those chairs, Niko. She's even got the springs coming out, and the stuffing, too. And the wretched bed and the awful, tiny kitchen wall. Oh, Emerald, this is truly amazing." She blinked in disbelief. "And the *broom* in the bucket! Now I know what happened to your hair."

"You have a gift," Niko complimented her

88

miserably. His voice was husky and dry, and though he smiled, his eyes looked sad.

"Angel's place is so tidy and cheerful by comparison," Darcy said.

"Anyplace would be cheerful by comparison," Niko murmured.

"You don't like it," Emerald said in a whisper.

"I like it," Niko answered. "I just wish it weren't *your* New York, Emerald. I'm so sorry."

"We're both so sorry," Darcy added in a choked voice. Then she turned away and blew her nose and didn't answer when Angel called, "Good-bye."

Emerald went back to her room to return the models to their ledge. She settled on her bed and opened her math book. But it was hard to concentrate. Through her half-open door she heard her parents' low voices.

"What have we done to her, Niko?" Darcy was saying. "While we selfishly run around chasing a career, making jokes about living like gerbils, she has suffered."

"It's not fair to her," Niko agreed. "She needs a place to grow up where there's light and air and space."

"Water Gap," Darcy said, as if that summed it all up.

"Water Gap," Niko repeated. "No matter what they offer us, *Near to My Heart* is just pie in the sky. We have to think about Emerald for a change."

"Even if they call tomorrow and give us the parts," Darcy said.

"Even if they call tomorrow and give us the parts," Niko echoed.

But they didn't hear the next day or Wednesday or Thursday. "Angel thinks her charm is broken," Emerald said. "It fell on the floor when she was asleep."

"That's all right," Darcy said. "We don't care about *Near to My Heart*. It's Water Gap for us. Anyway, this is Friday the thirteenth, so it's just as well we have no news."

"Friday the thirteenth has always been my good-luck day," Niko told her. "Whatever happens will be for the best."

Back in her room, Emerald carefully placed Stucksville and Montero World into shopping bags, hoping today would be her good-luck day as well.

"Are you taking those clever projects of yours to school?" Darcy asked as Emerald let herself out the door.

"They're due today."

"So soon?" Darcy ran her fingers through her long hair and laughed nervously. "I can't imagine what your teacher will make of them."

"Good luck," Niko called to her from the bathroom, where he was shaving.

On the stairs, Emerald met Angel. They rang Guthry's doorbell, and he came out carrying Guthry's Place in a large box.

"My dad says this is the strangest-looking essay he ever saw," Guthry said, looking worried.

"What's wrong with that?" Angel demanded.

Guthry didn't answer.

On the stoop, Grandma Diaz was arriving with her arms full of groceries. "What's in the bags?" she asked cheerfully.

"Essays," Guthry said, looking sideways at Angel, who glared into space.

"What's in the bags?" Mrs. Alter asked as they entered the classroom.

"Our New York," Emerald said.

"His, mine, and hers," Angel added.

Mrs. Alter peered into the bags at the boxes and frowned. "But the project was an essay, not a thing in a shopping bag."

"This is kind of an essay," Angel explained.

"*Kind* of an essay?" Mrs. Alter repeated. "There is no such thing. An essay is an essay. A rule is a rule. You didn't follow the rules for this assignment."

As they headed back to their seats, Hector pulled on Emerald's sleeve. "What's in the bags?" he whispered.

"Be still," Mrs. Alter scolded, glaring at Emerald.

"Trouble," Emerald answered Hector.

Mrs. Alter collected all the essays and stacked them on her desk next to the shopping bags. "During the week, the fourth-grade teachers will read all the essays to decide on the winners. The three winning essays will be read at assembly. The first-prize winner will be entered in the city-wide competition. For those of you who are late, we will consider an extension depending upon your reason. Any questions?"

"What's in the bags?" Denise called out.

"What's in the box?" Manny said.

"Oh, dear." Mrs. Alter eyed the bags and the box with a look of annoyance. "How I wish we didn't need to know." Then, taking a deep breath, she leaned over her desk and lifted them out one at a time to stack beside the pile of essays. "They are the work of some students," she said, frowning at the models as she spoke, "who didn't follow the rules of the contest."

Rules or no rules, the others were standing up in their seats for a better view. "Hey, what do you call that?" and "How'd you do that?" and "What's that?" they cried.

For a moment Mrs. Alter put her head in her hands, then, wearily, she looked over at Angel and Emerald and Guthry. "Okay, okay, I suppose you owe your classmates some explanation," she said.

Angel marched to the front desk, as if she could hardly wait to tell her story. "This here is Montero World," she announced, proudly pointing to her model. "With Stucksville and Guthry's Place, it's *our* New York—me, Emerald, and Guthry. It's where we live."

"You live in shoe boxes?" Denise taunted, and everyone laughed.

"Hush," Mrs. Alter ordered.

"Our place is rooms lined up," Angel persisted. "I live here in Five-A with my mother and father and my sister and my two brothers." She held up each doll in turn. "We got the place because my pop is super of the building."

"Super of shoe boxes," Manny teased.

"Quiet down, or else," Mrs. Alter threatened.

"Emerald calls her place Stucksville, because her mom says they planned to move into something bigger, but since their jobs didn't work out, they couldn't. So they are good and stuck."

"You can say that again," Denise agreed. "What a mess!"

"It's bigger than when we lived with my aunt and uncle after we had a fire," Margot said. "But we kept things supertidy, or my mom said we would go crazy."

"My family, we were in a single room until we moved into the project," Hector offered.

"It's amazing how you got everything to fit in so teeny-tiny," Lisa marveled. "It's like there's no space for one more thing. Is that why you never invited anybody over?"

Emerald found it odd to be the center of attention with everybody craning their necks to get a closer look. Odder still to find out that nobody was too surprised by how little space they had. "Our place is half an apartment that was divided up," she said, eager to tell them more now that they seemed so interested. "The back half. We look out on the courtyard. The big room has everything in it except my room, which my mother calls Cubby with Cot. In the Everything Room there is the kitchen, bedroom, living room, and dining room."

"But look how much space Guthry's got," Hector noted. "Look how nice it is."

"My folks knocked down some walls to make it big enough for them to live and work at home."

Now the whole class was crowding around the desk. "How did you make those chairs?" "Look at the bed that can fold up." "Could you show us how you did that?" "Hey, Mrs. Alter, could we all make models, too? Like at the museum?"

Mrs. Alter stood up, lifted the models off her desk, and put them away. "Everybody sit," she ordered. "You will leave all the projects here for the other fourth-grade teachers to see and judge.

I cannot guarantee that students who clearly didn't follow the rules can enter the contest."

Emerald felt a sharp poke in her side. "Did you hear that?" Guthry whispered.

Emerald nodded. She could see the back of Angel's neck. It seemed to be getting redder and redder. It was so red that Emerald hoped she'd never turn around.

She did, however, whenever she had a chance.

Frowning and glaring and pinching her lips together, she displayed her anger. It was a lucky thing she couldn't speak. At least not during class. "What's the big deal about following the rules all of a sudden?" she exploded on the way home from school. "They're allowing Lisa to do her Dance of the City instead of an essay. Why not our models?"

"I told you it wasn't an essay," Guthry said. "And now it's too late."

"Maybe it's not too late," Emerald argued. "Mrs. Alter said we could have an extension, if there was a good reason."

"So write an essay," Angel snapped. "I tried, and I can't. I told you, I'm good at talking and ideas. But when I put them on a page, they go bad on me."

"I only write things that fit inside a balloon over one of my comic characters' heads." Guthry told them. *"Bam, wham.* Put down that weapon." He thought for a moment. "I don't write on lined paper," he added.

They both looked at Emerald. "You got a good grade on that book report last fall," Angel remembered.

"Book reports are easy. You just tell what happened in the book. You don't have to make something up fresh."

"Maybe the other teachers will tell Mrs. Alter it's okay for us to enter the contest," Guthry said with a shrug. "Maybe they'll decide we should at least be in it, even if we can't win it."

"But I want to win." Angel stamped her foot. "Somebody's got to write an essay."

Emerald turned her head away.

Climbing up the stairs, they were surprised to hear laughter coming from someone's apartment. Emerald was sure it wasn't hers. But when she opened the door, Darcy and Niko jumped up from the table-trunk, which was set with a plate of crackers spread with tiny dabs of red caviar.

"Near to My Heart?" Emerald asked, her own heart doing a flip-flop.

Darcy shook her head. "We still haven't heard from them, but Water Gap liked our audition and made an offer. They've invited us to fly down and take a look."

"So it's celebration time!" Niko swooped Emerald off her feet and twirled her around. "If we want the jobs we shall have them. Meet the two new cast members of the Water Gap Theater."

"What about *Near to My Heart?*"

Darcy glanced over at the pile of real-estate catalogs and frowned. "Even if they took us, it would just be Stucksville plus."

"This is an expensive town," Niko explained. "Darcy has finally come to understand that." With a dramatic gesture he uncorked a chilled bottle of champagne and poured the pale liquid into a pair of juice glasses. He passed Emerald a cracker with caviar on top. "Do you know what this means?"

"It means no more Cubby with Cot," Darcy said softly. "It means the house and yard you've dreamed of. It means a real home so that you can work and play and invite friends to visit without being ashamed of where you live."

"It means we better call the airline and arrange for our flight down," Niko added. He picked up the phone and began to dial.

Emerald ate her cracker slowly, listening while her parents excitedly made plans. She wondered why she wasn't as happy as they were. For one thing, she had heard them celebrate like this before. Just before coming to New York, they had made a party for all their friends. They talked about "taking the Big Apple by storm" and being "overnight sensations." About winning Tony awards and Obies and turning into "household names."

She finished her cracker and went to her room. The window ledge was empty where Stucksville and Montero World had been. Feeling empty herself, Emerald raised the shade and stared across the courtyard at the fire escape, where Mrs. Farmer's old orange cat, Oz, seemed to be stuck on the metal slats, nearly frozen. The window that was sometimes open had been closed. Emerald's heart began to bang with excitement. She reached for her notebook page of telephone numbers. After four rings a drowsy voice answered.

"Your cat's on the fire escape and can't get back inside," Emerald whispered. Then she hung up and watched the window open. A shaggy head leaned out. "Kitty, kitty, kitty," Emerald heard through the glass panes. Then Oz slithered inside, and the window was quickly closed.

Emerald fell back on her bed.

4, she wrote. *Rescuer of Cats.* Then she closed the notebook and put it under her pillow.

Saving Oz the cat's life. Moving to Water Gap. In spite of everything that had happened in school, maybe Niko was right. Friday the thirteenth had been her personal good-luck day.

But if it was, she wondered why she was so sad about it.

Rule Breakers

"**S**omebody called Mrs. Farmer to tell her Oz was on the fire escape," Angel's voice thundered into the telephone early Saturday morning.

"Somebody called Grandma Diaz to tell her the baby was under the bed." Angel paused for a deep breath. "My brother Tony thinks it's the same somebody who squealed to my mother about Martin's superhero doll. You have any ideas about who that somebody is?"

"No." Emerald shook her head even though she was on the telephone. "I've got to go."

"If I were that somebody, I would make sure

I'd tell my best friend, especially if that best friend was wondering if somebody was spying on her and her whole family through the window in the courtyard." Angel paused. "Think about it," she concluded, giving Emerald something to do for the whole weekend.

Darcy and Niko were waiting. They were going to meet Molly and Saul for brunch and take in a show.

"Two days of treats," Darcy had said. "Something to celebrate the Water Gap offer. We've got real jobs now. No more 'What if?'"

But now it was Emerald who had what-ifs. Her spying had been a secret from everyone, but Angel seemed to have figured it out. They were supposed to be teammates. What if Angel was really angry that she'd been spying on her? Could she still look out the window? Would Angel still be her friend?

For two days of treats she tried to tell herself it didn't matter. "Outta here in less than a year," she mumbled to herself. But for the first time this did not make her feel any better.

"Outta here in less than a year," she repeated under her breath on Monday as she carefully chose a seat at the other end of the lunch table from Angel. "Outta here in less than a year," she chanted, avoiding Guthry's long stare.

"Are you talking to yourself?" Lisa Guzzman asked, plopping into the empty seat beside her.

"Just humming," Emerald stammered.

"I'd like to visit your house," Lisa said, unwrapping her sandwich. "I want to see how it really looks in Stucksville."

Emerald watched Lisa chew. She didn't know what to say.

"Listen, Emerald"—Lisa leaned toward her—"I could never tell, are you shy or stuck-up? I always thought stuck-up. But now I see you're shy. You could visit my place sometime. I share a room with my sister, and we are pretty squeezed. But now I see how it is. You are more squeezed for space than me."

"We're squeezed," Emerald managed to croak, "but I could fit you in."

"How about this afternoon?" Lisa suggested. "I have a little time before my ballet class."

"This afternoon?" Darcy and Niko had rushed off to do another audition for *Near to My Heart,* even though they had said they weren't really interested. Had they left a sink full of dishes? Were there clothes all over the chairs?

"Great," Lisa grinned, as if Emerald's shocked silence was an answer. "Later, I'll walk home with you."

But later Angel plunked down beside Emerald. "Lisa Guzzman just wants to see what a dump you live in. Remember, she can dance, but I'm your partner, whether we qualify or not."

This was not just the bad Angel, but the jealous Angel as well.

When school was out, Angel walked with Emerald and Lisa. "We're a team," she reminded Emerald. "Where you go, I go."

"I would ask you over—" Emerald began.

"So why don't you?"

"We haven't the room."

"Yes, you do. You just want Lisa for yourself." Good, bad, or jealous, when Angel spoke the truth, there was no arguing with her.

As they trudged up the five flights of stairs, Lisa began to gush, "Everybody loves your little boxes. Everybody thinks Mrs. Alter should qualify you even though the project didn't follow the rules."

"Like she qualified your Dance of the City," Angel huffed. "That's no essay."

"My Dance of the City?" Lisa repeated. "I wrote an essay. You think Mrs. A-Rule-Is-a-Rule Alter would let me just get up there and perform? You think I would have done all this work on my routine without permission? You think I'm stupid?"

Angel pinched her lips together and said nothing.

When Emerald opened the door, Darcy was curled up on the Murphy bed, going over her *Near to My Heart* script. "Hey," she greeted them absently, waving the script. "They want us to reaudition tomorrow."

Lisa's large eyes traveled from one corner of the room to the other, back and forth, up and down. "This is amazing," she marveled. "Does that bed really fold into the wall?"

"I'd let you do it." Darcy laughed. "But you'd have to fold me up as well."

"Why didn't you go for a sofa bed?"

"Because they didn't have one at the Goodwill Store," Darcy answered. "And where would we have put those?" She pointed to the easy chairs.

"Oh, look! The springs on the floor!" Lisa clapped her hands with delight. "Just like the model."

"I guess your project was a hit," Darcy said to

Emerald. "Even if it doesn't win, you could get it on TV. *Apartment Buildings of the Poor and Downtrodden.*"

"Poor and downtrodden?" Angel repeated, frowning.

"I know, I know," Darcy apologized. "Built like a fort and runs like a Swiss watch."

"You could use some nice stuff," Lisa told Darcy.

"They could use the rest of the apartment," Angel said. "Five-D."

"We're moving to Water Gap," Darcy told them. "There's no point in taking more space. There isn't even any point in auditioning for this soap opera. It's just a waste of time."

In Cubby with Cot, Lisa approved of the little rug. "Oh, I love that," she exclaimed over the vase. "It matches. If you got bunk beds you could do sleepovers. Also, you could put shelves around the top of the wall for extra storage. That way your parents could pick up some of the mess on the floor and put it away." She looked around, clicking her tongue in disapproval. "This place is small, but you haven't done as much as you could with it."

"You mean she could shrink," Angel hooted.

"I mean platforms and drawers and shelves and bunk beds," Lisa explained. "That's what I mean." She glanced at her watch and headed to the front door. "Good-bye, Mrs. Costos." She waved to Darcy. "I have to go to my dance class. Good luck with the auditions. I know how hard it is to do callbacks. But my agent always says it's better than no word at all." She turned to Emerald. "Next time, you come to my place. I'll give you some more good ideas."

"How about me?" Angel said, demanding equal time. "I could use a couple of ideas myself."

"You should write an essay to go with the model," Lisa advised. "That's the best idea I can think of."

After the door closed on Angel and Lisa, Darcy shook her head. "Her *agent,*" she bristled. "That little know-it-all. Just wait till you send her a picture of your new house in Water Gap."

"She's not a know-it-all," Emerald muttered. "She just thinks we could do more with this place. And she's right."

"When I want *House Beautiful,* I'll pick up a copy at the newsstand," Darcy snapped, before turning back to her script.

. . .

It wasn't until Thursday morning that Mrs. Alter summoned Emerald, Guthry, and Angel to her desk. "I've spoken with the other fourth-grade teachers. Unfortunately we cannot let your project qualify for the contest. It is not an essay. A rule is a rule, and learning to follow rules is as important as the project itself. Even as important as creating something new."

Emerald was speechless. How could it be that following rules was as important as creating something new and amazing? She couldn't bring herself to look at Angel. It was bad enough hearing her yelp of disappointed surprise.

"I won't give you a failing grade because you made a big effort in your own way and did a fine job," Mrs. Alter went on. "Your model will be on display at our school assembly so everyone can admire it. You will each receive a passing D."

As they returned to their seats, Margot whispered, "I think yours are the best. Everybody does."

"Everybody except the fourth-grade teachers," Angel said miserably.

"You made something that's just as good as

what we saw at the museum," Lisa told Emerald at lunch. "You shouldn't feel bad about it. Tell Angel."

On the way home from school, waiting on the curb for a light to change, Emerald did tell Angel. "Lisa says we made something as good as what we saw in the museum and we shouldn't feel bad about it," she said.

"We shouldn't feel bad about it?" Angel hollered. "Who says I feel bad about it?" She stopped speaking suddenly. "I swallowed funny." She covered her mouth. Tears streamed down her cheeks.

Guthry pulled a squashed roll of caramels from his pocket, but she shook her head and pushed them away.

Emerald offered a paper napkin left over from lunch.

"I don't need that," Angel sputtered, thrusting off the napkin. "I am *not* crying. I don't cry. Crying is for dopes and losers."

"Lisa is right," Emerald said. "We did make something like at the museum, and we shouldn't feel bad about it."

"We shouldn't feel bad about it?" Angel sniffled. "What do you care? You're outta here. But me?" Her eyes brimmed over. "Me and Guthry." She turned to him. "We're here. We care."

"You and Guthry," Emerald burst out. "I was part of the team, did you forget?"

"She was the part of the team that made me a part of the team," Guthry piped up in Emerald's defense. "But it was your idea that the models were essays without words, and we believed you."

"I tried to write something." Angel reached into her backpack and took out a wrinkled piece of notebook paper and handed it to Emerald. "My New York, the essay."

It didn't take Emerald two sentences to see that Angel's New York might be great, but her essay was awful. She handed the page back without a word.

"I tried, too," Guthry said, taking the spiral notebook he'd used at lunch out of his pocket. It was open to a new comic. The superhero was a character called Rule Breaker. He had wings and a magic pencil and saved the heroine, Ruby Jewel, by slipping new rules into the Rule King's Rule Book. Ruby Jewel, Emerald was delighted to no-

110

tice, had large dark eyes and long hair with a few strands sticking straight up on top, as if they were cropped off to make a very tiny broom. "It came out a comic strip."

She handed Rule Breaker back to Guthry. "It's great," she said.

"But it's not an essay," Angel wailed.

They both looked at Emerald.

"Why should she bother?" Angel said to Guthry. "In another year she's outta here."

It was a dreary cold afternoon. Old snow lay in hard, dirty piles at the edge of the sidewalk. They stepped carefully so as not to slip on icy patches. "Less than a year," Emerald corrected Angel.

"Less than a year," Angel repeated. "Your dream will come true."

If this was so, Emerald wondered, why did she wish Rule Breaker could really save her? Why did she feel so bad?

Cherries Emerald

"Buenos dias," Mr. Chef greeted them on the stoop. He was returning home with large bags of food.

"Buenos dias," Emerald mumbled as Angel and Guthry flew past her and up the steps.

"The girl in the window," he said. "And the boxes in the window." He smiled under his mustache. "It made my wife happy to see those nice models. We miss them."

Emerald was amazed. It had not occurred to her that both she and their work could be seen by so many people. "The boxes were a project. We had to take them to school."

"Yes, a contest." Mr. Chef nodded knowingly. "Mrs. Montero told me all about it. We want to wish you good luck and tell you that after you win first prize, please put them in the window again."

Once she was in the apartment, Emerald went to her room and closed the door. Everyone knew about the contest. Now everyone would have to know that they didn't even qualify. Darcy and Niko would say, Oh, poor pet. So sorry. These things happen. But soon we're off to Water Gap, and it will all be a memory. Only right now it wasn't a memory. It was fresh and real.

Emerald lay back on her pillow and gazed up at the ceiling. The brown spot was bigger than ever. Maybe it was a water spot and soon there would be a leak. Then, to her surprise, it wasn't the ceiling that started to spring a leak. Though it took her by surprise, she could understand why Angel had been in tears.

She sat up and lifted her shade, hoping for some really interesting scenes—Lenore trying out a new dance step, or one of Angel's brothers getting into trouble. Except for the Montero kitchen and the Professor's reading lamp, the courtyard windows were blank. After a while the light went on in Mr. and Mrs. Chef's kitchen. Because of his job, the Chefs ate a very early dinner. Soon there were pots on the stove and chopping and stirring and steam rising from a casserole. In a separate bowl on the table, Mr. Chef poured out a liquid, and then, as if it were magic, the liquid turned into fire and flared up so high, it was nearly to the top of the window. Emerald gasped. The flame was blue-white, soaring and rippling around the dish and filling the entire window.

Police! Fire!

Lucky for her, Darcy had left important numbers under a magnet on the fridge. Emerald reached for the phone and dialed.

In no time she heard sirens wailing and heavy boots and loudspeakers on the stairway. Everyone in the building who had been hanging out the window was now rushing onto their landings and down the stairs. The Monteros, the Lauffers, Mrs. Piano, even Mrs. Farmer and Oz.

The fire marshal banged on Mr. Chef's door.

"It's my cherries jubilee!" he cried.

"But who called?"

"Who could have seen?"

"Who could have known?"

"The girl in the window," Grandma Diaz said with a knowing smile, glancing up from her landing on the floor below. "She sees everything."

All heads turned toward Emerald, who had been standing silently in her open door. She felt as if the flames from the cherries jubilee had swept up from Mr. Chef's kitchen to engulf her.

Mr. Montero shook his head. "Lucky they didn't break down the door. That would have cost us."

"It already has," the fire marshal told him. "Every time we answer an alarm, it's many dollars of taxpayers' money."

It had cost Emerald as well as the taxpayers. Not in dollars, but in something she could hardly put a name to.

She turned her flaming face away from the group of neighbors who had gathered on landings and stairs. If she could have disappeared in an instant, she would have done so. Instead she slipped back into apartment 5C and closed the door behind her.

As soon as they came home, Niko and Darcy ran up the steps. "Everybody's downstairs talking about the fire," Darcy said breathlessly. "Now that I know you're okay, let's go back. It's such a drama, I want to hear more."

"I'd rather not," Emerald begged off.

"Oh, come on, sweetheart." Niko pulled her out of the easy chair where she had crumpled like unsorted laundry. "This is the kind of story you'll be telling your new classmates in Water Gap."

When Emerald didn't budge, Niko and Darcy, still laughing, pulled her by the hand, through the door and down the steps to the first-floor landing, where everyone had gathered to discuss what had happened. Mrs. Chef described it as a great drama. Mrs. Lauffer said it was "one for the books." Mr. Chef boasted that he had prepared the most expensive cherries jubilee in history. Mrs. Farmer said she knew now who had told her Oz was on the fire escape. Grandma Diaz knew who had found the baby under the bed. Angel's brother Tony glared at Emerald. "I know something, too," he growled. Angel was silent for a long time. She looked like a darkening sky just before a hurricane.

Finally she said, "I thought we were partners. I thought we were a team. I shared with you. I told you about my jobs in the building. I told you everything, and all the time you had secrets."

"Cheer up, darling." Darcy reached out to take Emerald by the hand and draw her back upstairs. "One day this will all blow over and make a funny story to tell new friends in your new school."

"Here's another funny story," Emerald said, trying to hold back her tears. "Our project didn't qualify. We won't be part of the contest. There's no such thing as an essay with no words."

"That's not a funny story," Darcy agreed, pulling back Emerald's hair from her forehead and kissing her gently. "That's bad news."

And there was more bad news. Friday morning, Angel was not waiting to walk to school. She had left early enough to inform everyone in the class about Emerald's cherries jubilee.

"Woooo, woooo." Hector greeted Emerald with fire engine sounds as she entered the classroom.

"How do you make cherries Emerald?" Denise called out. "Add rum and call the fire department."

"Leave her alone," Guthry growled. He picked up his pencil as if it were a weapon and opened his notebook. "Or I'll draw you in a way you'll never forget."

Denise clapped a hand over her mouth and fell back into her seat.

"Okay, okay. Hush," Mrs. Alter scolded over the laughter.

Emerald wrapped herself in something she called her miraculous miracle cloak. This cloak, she decided, made her invisible. Whenever she was about to leave a school, she would put it on and pretend she was already gone. All she had to do was stop raising her hand in class and remember to look the other way if anyone spoke to her or tried to catch her eye. In the school yard she leaned against the metal railing and pretended to be part of it. At lunch she sat as far from her classmates as the crowded table would allow, imagining the border of pansies she would plant in her backyard in Water Gap.

"What you got in your lunch?" Margot called out. "Hot chilies? Call the firemen."

"Stucksville is burning," Denise teased when she saw that Guthry was not paying attention.

"She doesn't need the firemen," Angel said. "She'd like it if the place burned down. She's outta here in a year."

Forgetting she was invisible, Emerald glared

into Angel's black-olive eyes. "That's right," she said, "I am."

"Too bad." Guthry looked up and smiled. "We could have been the Designing Dynamos, Inc. We could have done the whole building, the whole street. Other people's buildings, other people's streets." His eyes glowed. "We could have made a business corporation like my parents."

When she got home from school that afternoon, Emerald found Darcy's collection of real-estate catalogs in the pile of papers to recycle. She dusted them off and took them into her room. After making sure that her shade was drawn, she settled on her bed with Elite Properties. She turned the pages slowly, trying to imagine life in the city in eight rooms with wood-burning fireplace and views . . . with marble lobbies and thick carpets and elevators with benches in them and doormen in uniforms. After a while she imagined houses in the suburbs behind gated gardens and lawns, and schools that sent buses. She imagined until her head grew achy and her eyes tired. She heard Darcy and Niko return from their third callback audition for *Near to My Heart.* They were cooking in the Everything Room.

"Real food for a change," she heard Niko say. "There won't be any more takeout in Water Gap."

"No more blinis with caviar?" Darcy sighed in fake sorrow.

"No more pâté with truffles." Niko pretended to sob.

"And not a moment too soon," Darcy concluded in her own voice. "It's time to move on. Our little girl needs a house and garden. Not Cubby with Cot with a brick wall and fire escape for scenic view. It's time we stop thinking of our careers and give Emerald what she's always wanted."

What she always wanted? Water Gap? The words made her feel as if a heavy load had settled on her chest.

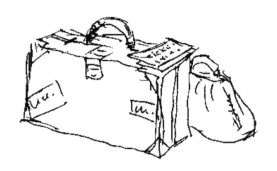

Escape to Water Gap

"What's this about?" Mrs. Alter asked when Emerald handed her a note from Darcy asking that she be dismissed early.

"We have to catch a plane to Water Gap," Emerald explained loudly, hoping her voice would carry so the whole class would hear. "To make plans for when we move."

"Moving again?" Mrs. Alter glanced at Emerald, who fidgeted uncomfortably at the side of her desk.

"We'll be leaving soon." Emerald nodded, try-ing not to look at Angel or Guthry.

"You have permission to be excused at a quarter of." Mrs. Alter folded the note and returned it to her. "But whether you move or stay, Emerald, you will either be a person who listens and follows the rules or a person who daydreams and doesn't care. Moving won't change who you are."

Emerald hung her head, deciding the best person to be at the moment was one wrapped in a miraculous miracle cloak.

"So tune in," Mrs. Alter advised. "Just remember, we can all see you, even if you choose not to see us."

If everyone could see her, as Mrs. Alter said, she wondered why Angel had stopped walking to school with her and why Lisa had never come through with her invitation. Only Guthry continued to even look in her direction. His smile of encouragement made her want to cry.

In her new school she would make sure she did her work and avoided classmates.

When she got home, Darcy and Niko were waiting with their suitcase. "We'll have a snack on the plane," Darcy said as they hurried downstairs to find a taxi that would take them to the airport.

The flight was just long enough for juice and

crackers and scalding tea. When the plane landed, a brilliant sunset painted the sky in gold and pink and deep purple. "A good omen," Niko told them on the drive to the motel.

The next morning they all went to visit the Water Gap Theater, which was in an old building that had once been an opera house. It had gilt boxes and a ceiling covered with angels. While Niko and Darcy ooohed and ahhhhed, Emerald sat in the second row of the half-dark theater, half-listening to her parents' conversation with the theater manager up on the stage. She remembered all the theaters where she had waited while her parents rehearsed or performed. After a while she opened one of the books Darcy had packed for her and tried to read, but the light was dim and her mind kept wandering. What would it be like to live here? She would attend a new school. There would be new classmates, new teachers, new rules.

When Niko and Darcy returned from their meeting, they went to lunch with a member of the cast. He drove them around so they could see the neighborhoods.

"Here's where most of us in the company live."

He pointed out a street of neat houses, each with a yard and fence and back patio. "They're small but pleasant homes."

"Small?" Darcy laughed. "Our current abode is a box that once contained Niko's cowboy boots." She winked at Emerald.

On the plane ride home, Niko and Darcy discussed the future. "It seems they can't commit to more than a year," Niko warned. "If we take these jobs, we give up the chance to be in *Near to My Heart,* and in another year we might have to pull up stakes again."

"We'll worry about that when the time comes." Darcy glanced in Emerald's direction. "We have to remember what's important. *Near to My Heart* does not include a backyard."

Niko nodded and reached over to give Emerald a hug along with his big Groucho Marx smile. "How about that backyard, sweetheart?"

"I'm not sure," Emerald said, recalling the flat patch of dull ground with a fence around it.

"It will be green in the summer," Niko assured her. "A big difference."

"That house had a patio," Darcy cried, as if it were a swimming pool and tennis court.

Emerald felt hopeless. How could she explain

to them what she didn't understand herself? She gazed out the window at a passing cloud. "I should worry, I should care," she whispered.

"There, that's the spirit." Darcy laughed with relief, and Emerald knew she was their little trouper again.

When they got back to New York it was Sunday late afternoon. Niko paid the cab driver and carried their baggage up the five flights of stairs. Darcy emptied out their suitcase and headed off to the Laundromat across the street. Niko went to run some errands and buy groceries and a take-out dinner.

"Be back before you've done your homework," Darcy said, waving from the door.

Emerald sat on her bed and opened her notebook to the last page, where she had written

Cases
1. Superhero Locator.
2. Baby Finder.
3. Matchmaker.
4. Rescuer of Cats.

Her list ended there. She had never listed *Firefighter* but decided to do it now. After all, that had been her intention. But when she saw the word, it made her even sadder. She hadn't looked out of her window since the day Mr. Chef made cherries jubilee. Now, in spite of herself, she lifted the shade and peered out. What did it matter? She would be moving soon.

Montero World was packed with visitors. It looked as if a birthday party was just starting. There were presents and party hats on the table. Lenny Lauffer was there as well. On the floor below, Mrs. Piano was at her piano. Two floors down, the Professor was reading his paper under the yellow lamp. Slowly Emerald began to feel better.

After a while Darcy came in. Emerald heard her singing to herself as she folded their laundry. At six o'clock Darcy turned on the news. Emerald waited for the Professor to turn off his lamp. When he didn't budge, she noticed that the paper had slipped to the floor and his head was at a tilt. He must be sleeping, Emerald thought. She yawned. She was drowsy, too. Her eyes began to close. She drew her quilt up over her knees and put her head on the pillow.

When she awoke, Darcy was tapping on the

door. "I'm off to do another load of wash," she said. "When I get back, Niko should be home with dinner."

Emerald sat up. She glanced out her window again. The Monteros were sitting down to dinner. Mrs. Piano was no longer at the piano. But the Professor was still in his chair under the yellow lamp. His head was still at the same odd tilt, and the paper was still on the floor. It seemed to Emerald that he had not moved at all. Was something wrong? Her heart began to pound. What should she do? Without thinking, she reached for her notebook and turned to the page of the neighbors' telephone numbers that she had vowed never to use again. As the Professor's phone rang over and over in her ear, she could practically hear it from across the courtyard. The ringing phone and her thudding heart filled her head with noise. Five, six, seven, eight times it rang, but still Professor Hahn didn't budge. Emerald let the plastic receiver slip from her hand onto its cradle. What now? She had learned enough not to call fire and police. Then she remembered that Angel had told her Guthry's parents kept Professor Hahn's key.

Emerald headed down the stairs. On the first floor, she rang the Lauffers' bell and then banged impatiently on the door. "Guthry," she shouted. "It's Emerald."

She heard footsteps. "When nobody's home, I'm not allowed to open."

"Then I'm Ruby Jewel, and you're Rule Breaker."

Guthry turned the latch and slid the bolt. He peered out through the narrow space. "What's up?"

"Professor Hahn. He hasn't moved from his chair in hours. I called him, but he didn't answer. He didn't budge. I let it ring and ring. And the TV is still on and it's after six."

Guthry took the chain off its hook. "What do you want me to do?"

"We have to check him out." Emerald said, stepping over the threshold. "Find the key."

It seemed to take forever till Guthry returned from the kitchen with a ring of color-coded keys. Together they ran up the stairs. Then he rang the Professor's bell. When there was no answer and he had called out a few times, he inserted the key in the latch and turned it this way and that. "Sticks," Guthry said, his face shiny with sweat.

Emerald was about to snatch it from his hand for a try of her own when the lock turned and they pushed the door open.

New Beginnings

Inside the Professor's apartment was the familiar long dark corridor, ending in a room with the yellow lamp, newspaper, books, and the Professor himself, limp as a rag doll in his armchair, his face still and waxy. The pages of the newspaper had fallen all about him, and his eyes were closed.

"Get Mr. Montero, quick," Guthry gasped.

Emerald ran up the stairs and banged on the Monteros' door.

Then everything happened in a rush. Mr. Montero at his door, with a piece of Lenore's birthday cake in one hand. Lenny and Angel and Mrs. Montero rising from the table behind him. Mrs. Piano, Mr. and Mrs. Chef, and the Diaz family all on the landing to ask what had happened. The ambulance and the men who came with a stretcher. Darcy returning with the laundry. Niko carrying bags of groceries and take-out dinners. The Professor opening his eyes briefly and then closing them before being placed in the ambulance.

Emerald saw Guthry's parents running toward the crowd that had gathered on the pavement.

Mrs. Lauffer hugged Guthry. "When we saw the ambulance from the corner," she said, "I thought I would need one, too."

"It's lucky Guthry had the key," Mrs. Piano said. "Otherwise they would have had to break down the door."

"Guthry?" Mr. Lauffer turned to his son. "But how did you know Professor Hahn was ill?"

Mrs. Lauffer took her husband by the elbow. "How do you think?" she asked, and they both answered together: "Emerald."

Mr. Lauffer went to ride in the ambulance with the Professor. The other tenants lingered on the stoop.

"He must have had a heart attack."

"A stroke."

"A seizure."

Angel pulled Emerald aside. "Why didn't you come to my door first?" she asked, her hands on her hips, her eyes blazing. "How come you went to Guthry?"

"For one thing, he had the key," Emerald answered. Then, meeting Angel's eyes, she added, "And for another, no matter what happened, he wouldn't tease me about it afterward."

"Such a person should not live alone." Mrs. Montero shook her head disapprovingly. "Or he should have one of those little alarms you wear around your neck."

Mrs. Piano began to laugh. "He didn't need a little alarm around his neck. He had a big alarm watching him from across the courtyard."

"The girl in the window," Mr. Chef agreed. "She looks out for all of us."

"We're her TV show," his wife added. "Even if she doesn't always get the plot right, she stays tuned."

"You must be proud of her," Mrs. Lauffer said to Darcy and Niko.

"Actually"—Niko began to cough; he seemed to have something caught in his throat—"we had no idea."

"Ever since you moved in, I've wanted to invite you over," Mrs. Lauffer said to Darcy and Niko. "Our apartment is similar to what yours would be if it wasn't divided up"—she paused—"and we've done a lot of rearranging. Is this a good time?"

"None better," Darcy told her, with a glance at Niko, who nodded his agreement. So they all followed Guthry, and his parents through the first-floor door with its sign DESIGNS BY LAUFFER, INC.

Darcy gasped at her first sight of the large open space. "How did you do it?"

"With an architect's plan, a contractor, and a lot of headaches," Mrs. Lauffer said. "We use the apartment both for living and working. It saves a bundle." She led them into their kitchen, shiny with its steel sink and stove and white tile counters. "Won't you have something to drink?" She opened the fridge and reached for a bottle of soda.

"Please don't trouble," Darcy said. "I was about to make dinner."

"We've just come from a weekend in Water Gap," Niko explained. "We flew down to have a look at the theater where we'll be working next year. We've got a lot of planning and thinking to do."

"But you've only just moved in," Mrs. Lauffer exclaimed. "And now you're moving again?"

Darcy glanced at Emerald. "It's time we gave our little girl a break," she said softly.

"I don't understand."

"Did you happen to see her project for the My New York contest?"

Mrs. Lauffer shook her head. "Only Guthry's. It's a pity they didn't qualify. This idea that a rule is a rule seems too harsh. Sometimes good things happen when a rule gets bent."

"Emerald's model was made out of a boot box," Darcy said. "It had toothpaste-carton chairs with ballpoint-pen springs poking out. There were matchboxes to show our camp-trunk dining table and washcloths on the floor in place of our raggedy rugs. She made our Murphy bed out of a mirror with a makeup applicator for a mattress. She even folded it up into the wall, which it hardly ever is. She called the model Stucksville. That's our joke, but it's not so funny if you actually have to live in it. Maybe the model didn't qualify as an essay, but it told us plenty—and it's time we take her out of this."

Mrs. Lauffer seemed puzzled. "Out of this?"

Darcy looked around. "We live like shoes on a store shelf. One on top of the other. Stucksville."

"Stucksville?" Mrs. Lauffer repeated. She paused. And then she said, "You know, I grew up in this building. I like it here. I've liked raising my family here. I like to recognize my neighbors and the faces on the street. I like seeing how babies grow up and grown-ups grow old. I like seeing how the shops change hands and get bigger." She thought for a moment. "I like knowing there are people all around me whose lives are different and separate from my own, but who are connected to me somehow."

"We'd like a new beginning," Niko said.

"Sometimes new beginnings can happen if you stay home," Mrs. Lauffer argued. "We'll be sorry to see you go."

New beginnings again, Emerald thought, as she followed her parents up the four flights of stairs. New beginnings meant that she was always about to be smarter in her new school, her parents were always about to have the better roles in their new theater company. They were always about to have a great place to live. New beginnings meant you never had to find out what would have happened if you'd stayed longer.

Up in Cubby with Cot, she opened her notebook and under *5. Firefighter,* she wrote *6. Saving Professor Hahn.* She stared at the entry for a long time. "I should worry, I should care," she told herself. But the words gave her no comfort . . . because suddenly she *did worry* and she *did care.*

In another year, where she wanted to be was *here.*

"Dinner's on," Niko called into her room. "White beans and tuna casserole to celebrate Emerald. And Mrs. Lauffer called—the Professor's going to be okay."

"Three cheers for Emerald, the heroine of the day," Darcy added. "What a wonderful thing you did, sweetheart. We may be just passing through this place, but they'll never forget you."

"When we move to Water Gap you'll have something better to do with your time than just stare into windows across the courtyard. There won't be windows across the courtyard. There won't even be a courtyard. You'll have a real patio and a yard."

Emerald took a deep breath. "I have to tell you something."

"Yes, my love," Niko said, taking the casserole off the stove and setting it down on the trunk with great care.

"I want to live here. I don't want to move to Water Gap."

"You mean no house and yard?"

"No house and yard in Water Gap." She nodded. "You don't have to move for me. I want to stay."

Niko and Darcy exchanged glances the way they did when they were rehearsing their lines, telling each other something without speaking. "You're such a good little trouper," Darcy said gently, "you don't even know how to stick up for yourself."

"But I do."

"Emerald the jewel." Niko kissed the top of her head. "We saw the model, and we know what it means."

"No, you don't," she said hopelessly. How could she make them see she was telling the truth?

Back in Cubby with Cot, Emerald turned to the last page of her notebook and printed *7. Escape from Escape.* Then at the top of a new page she wrote *Dear Niko and Darcy.* At first the words came slowly, but soon her pen began to move across the page so quickly, it could scarcely keep up with her thoughts. She was hearing the words and had only to get them down. Suddenly writing was as simple as breathing. When she was done, she reread what she had written, crossed out *Dear Niko and Darcy,* and made a fresh copy. This wasn't a letter. It certainly wasn't a comic strip. But with a little luck, it might be an essay.

My New York

Emerald left for school early. She was the first in the classroom.

"I have something to give you," she said to Mrs. Alter, placing her pages on the desk.

"What's this?" Mrs. Alter asked.

"You'll see."

Other students were beginning to enter the room. Mrs. Alter tucked the pages into a folder.

"It will have to wait," she said.

And so would Emerald.

Emerald waited all week for a word or smile or nod from her teacher. None came. By Friday, the morning of the assembly, she decided the pages had been lost. Or perhaps it was too late for new pages. She put on a blue skirt Darcy had bought her for the weekend trip to Water Gap. They were to leave directly after the assembly, pick up their suitcase, and make a "mad dash" to the air-port and an early afternoon flight.

"We've got lots to do." Darcy had counted off the list on her fingers. "Find a house to rent. Register Emerald for a new school. Change bank accounts." It was a new beginning, all right.

Along with the skirt there was a matching turtleneck sweater. Emerald pulled it over her head and then lifted the neck so it covered her face right up to the top of her nose. If things got really bad, she could pull up her turtleneck. Along with the miraculous miracle cloak. She would be really gone. She slipped into her jacket and did up the toggles as slowly as possible.

Darcy kissed her good-bye distractedly. "See you later at the assembly."

Angel was waiting at the landing with a grim expression. On the first floor, Guthry stood just outside his door.

"Are your parents coming?" Emerald asked.

"Yes," Angel muttered miserably. "They thought I would be a winner."

"Mine are coming, too," Guthry said. "They don't care if we win or even qualify. They think we did a really great job. Lenny says I can use my project for a portfolio when I apply to the School of Art and Design. It will be a winner."

"A winner?" Angel scoffed. "How can you be a winner if you can't even compete?"

"Maybe there's more than one way to win," Guthry suggested.

"I never heard of it," Angel muttered.

Outside, the sky was light and clear over the tops of the buildings. Buckets of daffodils placed outside the markets appeared like yellow flags, announcing the season. Suddenly the strain that hung about them vanished, and all three broke into a run, whooping when they reached the curbs, laughing until they were breathless. By the time they arrived at school, they were holding their sides and gasping for air.

"Oh, wow," Angel cried as they entered the front lobby.

A huge MY NEW YORK banner had been hung on a rope from one wall to the other. Large posters illustrated by second and sixth graders were everywhere. The school looked as if it had been dressed for a party.

Since they would be dismissed right after the program, Mrs. Alter took attendance and had them line up in their jackets before filing down to the assembly. Inside the auditorium were more posters and drawings. But where was their project? Hadn't Mrs. Alter promised that it would be placed on display?

When all the classes were seated, Mrs. Bowdry, the music teacher, began to play chords on the piano, signaling the audience to be silent. Dr. Hurely, the principal, climbed onto the stage. "Welcome," she said into a microphone that whined and had to be adjusted. "We had such a good time working on these projects that we are eager to share them with family and friends. It gives me great pleasure to start our program with the third-grade presentation of an original skit."

The third grade's original skit was about Peter Minuit buying Manhattan Island from the Indians. Two students forgot their lines. One burst into tears and left the stage. Everybody stood up and applauded the entire third grade, but especially the student who had burst into tears.

"We should have cried," Angel growled. "All we had to do was cry, and we would have qualified."

When the stage was cleared, Lisa Guzzman performed her original Dance of the City.

"If you are cute and wear costumes or cry, you get anything you want," Angel hissed into Emerald's ear.

Mrs. Alter was still clapping as she walked up to the microphone. "You see what talent we have in our school. It was very hard for judges of the fourth-grade essay contest to choose only three winners. Every one of the entries had something to say. Every one of them was interesting. We certainly hope the essay we awarded first prize will win the citywide competition, but even if it doesn't, we have learned so much about our city and ourselves that we are all winners. It gives me great pleasure to end today's program with readings of the three prize essays."

She cleared her throat, and Angel sucked in her breath, making a sound like a broken vacuum cleaner. "Here goes nothing," she said.

"Hector Torres, third prize." Mrs. Alter smiled at the audience while Hector sidled out of his row and down the aisle, to his family's wild whoops and roars.

"'My Firehouse,'" Hector boomed. Mrs. Alter adjusted the mike and advised him to lower his voice. Hector lowered his voice but went so fast that Mrs. Alter suggested at the end that maybe he had been rushing to put out a blaze.

"Second prize," Mrs. Alter called from the podium, "Myrna Devenny."

Myrna Devenny, a tiny, shy girl with many long braids, read in a singsong voice about the community center that was so important to her neighborhood, and how they had just collected clothing for the victims of an earthquake in South America.

"She collected, all right," Angel snapped. "That's where she got her pink dress that she wore to Lisa's birthday party."

Mrs. Alter congratulated Myrna. "My New York," Mrs. Alter said slowly. "Celebrated by our students in posters, skits, a dance routine, and then . . . something none of us expected."

A hush fell on the auditorium. Emerald could sense that everyone was holding their breath.

Mrs. Bowdry walked onto the stage pushing a table. On it sat the models of Stucksville, Montero World, and Guthry's Place.

"Angel Montero, Emerald Costos, and Guthry Lauffer, neighbors in the same building, have created models of the apartments in which they live," Mrs. Alter said. "They were told that their models could not qualify for the contest since they were not essays."

Emerald was embarrassed to hear Angel hiss, "No fair."

"However"—Mrs. Alter held up the finger of one hand—"this week, at the last minute, Emerald submitted the words to go with the models, qualifying them as an essay with a model attachment. I will ask the three students to come up onto the stage and ask Emerald to read you the essay for which all of them shall share first prize."

Emerald seemed to be stuck to her seat. "You never tell me anything!" Angel burst out, giving her a shove. "Get up. Go."

With Angel just behind her, pushing and prodding as if she were an oversized Beanie Baby, Emerald found herself moving down the aisle and up to the podium, where Guthry stumbled to join them. Standing beside Mrs. Alter with the essay spread before her on the stand, she wondered if she would be able to read it. Half-wishing to escape, she looked out to the swinging doors at the back of the auditorium. Niko and Darcy had just come through.

"'Back in January,'" she began, startled by the sound of her booming, miked voice, "'our class visited the Museum of the City of New York. We saw model houses that showed how people lived in the city over a hundred years ago. This gave Angel the idea that we should make models of the places where we live for the My New York essay contest. She said it didn't matter if the places weren't fancy and rich. She said where we live is important. She said they tell a story, even if it's not in writing.

"'I told Angel she was wrong. A model isn't an essay, where we live isn't important, and where I live has no story. But Angel said she was going to do it anyway.'" Emerald looked out at the audience. "You know Angel," she said. There was a sound like a ripple of laughter.

"'Angel made her apartment, which is called

146

Montero World,'" Emerald continued, pointing to Angel's model. "'It tells how the Monteros came to New York from another country and filled their house with beds and cabinets and pots and pans and sofas so it would be a nice place for Angel and her sister and brothers to live. Mr. Montero is the building super. He makes sure that our building is like a fort and runs like a Swiss watch. Angel does jobs for tenants. She walks dogs and runs errands.

"'Guthry's Place'"—Emerald nodded in the direction of Guthry's box—"'is where his mother grew up. His parents fixed the apartment so it's full of space and light, and they can work in it while they live in it. Mrs. Lauffer says she likes to recognize her neighbors and the faces on the street. She likes to see how babies grow up and how grown-ups grow old, how shops change hands and get bigger. She likes to know that there are people all around her who are different and separate, but still connected to her.'" Emerald turned the page and took a deep breath.

"'My parents took one half of an apartment because they thought they would soon get good acting jobs and wouldn't stay long. When the

147

jobs didn't work out, they felt stuck.'" She looked out at the audience and placed a hand on top of the boot box. "Stucksville," she said.

To her surprise, there was another burst of laughter, followed by applause, as if she had just introduced something that was not only funny, but familiar.

"'Angel was right,'" she continued. "'Stucksville does tell a story. My father says everything in Five-C plays a couple of parts, like actors in a small company. The fold-up bed that has a mirror on the back is next to the refrigerator that also works as an alarm clock. The easy chairs with the springs and stuffing coming out are for sitting and for piling up the laundry, and the camp trunk that holds our summer clothes is also the table where we eat.

"'My window that faces the courtyard isn't just a window. It's a view into other worlds. At first, I just liked to look, as if it was a TV. It made me feel better when I was lonely. But then I saw things nobody else knew about. A cat stuck out on the fire escape. A baby sleeping under the bed while his grandma looked for him. A toy that fell off the window ledge.'" She paused. "'And once I called the fire department for something that turned out to be cherries jubilee.'" This time, there was an eruption of laughter.

"'When my parents saw my model, they thought it showed how miserable I am and how much I want to move. They couldn't believe me when I told them they were wrong. How could I explain to them that what my model shows is that I found out I have a New York after all, and that My New York is home?'"

Emerald folded up her pages and stepped back from them. Mrs. Alter directed her to line up with Guthry and Angel for a photograph and a fresh round of applause.

Mrs. Bowdry began to play a closing song, "The Sidewalks of New York." Angel linked her arms through Emerald's and Guthry's. She swayed to the music. "'East Side, West Side,'" she sang ecstatically. "I knew it was a good idea to team up." She pinched Emerald and grinned at Guthry. "And now we're going to win the big one and meet the mayor, just like I said."

Before she met the mayor, however, Emerald knew she would have to meet Darcy and Niko. They stood in front of the auditorium looking as if they were in the middle of a play for which they hadn't been given any lines.

"Congratulations," Darcy said. "Still waters run deep."

"She means, how come you didn't tell us how you felt?" Niko said.

"I tried. You thought I was acting."

Angel came up behind them. "Emerald pulled a fast one," she said.

"Rule Breaker and the Designing Dynamos, Inc." Guthry raised an arm in triumph. "We won."

"I thought you didn't care," Angel reminded him.

Angel, Emerald, and Guthry followed their parents down the aisle and through the swinging doors to the lobby and out onto the street.

"That was some wonderful work," Mrs. Montero congratulated them.

Mr. Lauffer pointed toward a pizzeria. "We're going for lunch. Will you all join us?"

Niko looked at his watch. "That sounds like a great idea."

"Aren't you flying down to Water Gap this afternoon?" Mrs. Lauffer asked.

Niko shook his head. "As it turns out, something better has come up in a new and more interesting place."

"A better offer? A new and more interesting place?" Emerald's heart sank.

"Where's that?" Mr. Lauffer asked.

"Five-C," Niko said.

"With D attached," Darcy added.

"Home." Niko took Emerald by the hand. "A place where you can make beds out of mirrors and bookcases out of matchboxes and, if you put your mind to it, find work and settle down. We've decided to take a chance on *Near to My Heart* and hope for the best."

Emerald noticed the tin sign twirling in the entrance to the pizzeria. The metal awning rattled in the wind. Inside was the smell of baking pizza in the ovens and rows of tables with shakers of pepper and salt. The manager was tossing out a small plastic Christmas tree that had decorated the cashier's counter all winter and replacing it with a pot containing a few plastic daffodils. "Spring," he told them.

Spring? So soon? It was hard to believe how much had changed since that cold day in January, when she had begun to understand that no matter how they lived, *where* they lived was important. Carefully she lifted the plastic tree from the top of the trash and tucked it into her knapsack.

Niko threw her a look. "More Stucksville?" he asked.

Emerald nodded and smiled. Five-D had a window, and outside the window there was a tree. Under the tree there was a street. On that street there were shops and stoops and . . . My New York, she thought. She could hardly wait.